FRANCES MURRAY

The Heroine's Sister

ST. MARTIN'S PRESS   NEW YORK

For Judy
who wanted to know
what happened next.

Contents

I

"O, shine Diamond!"

Tales of Hoffman: OFFENBACH

THE ORCHESTRA ROOM IN the Teatro Benedetto consisted of half
the space below the stage. Inside it was just possible to stand if
you were not particularly tall. Because the Campo Benedetto
was in Venice, the prevailing atmosphere was one of melancholy
damp. One winter morning in 1868 Eduardo Torcellano the
'cellist was busy in this orchestra room. He had as his assistant a
timid little violinist who suffered the unsuitable sobriquet of
Lupo, and who scurried to and fro like the apprentice-sorcerer's
broomstick. Their occupation seemed somewhat unmusical : on
the bench which ran round the walls of the room were a variety
of open instrument-cases, and Eduardo was engaged in packing
these tightly with bundles of pamphlets which Lupo fetched
from the room next door, where a muffled rhythmic thumping
proclaimed the presence of a small printing press. They were
interrupted in this activity by a loud double thump from the
stage above where the repétisseur had been rehearsing the four
principals in a quartette accompanied by a tinkling, elderly
pianoforte. Quickly, Eduardo slammed the cases shut and
latched them. Lupo shouted a word of warning into the other
room and the thudding ceased at once. The connecting door was
closed and the bolts shot on the inside. Eduardo pulled some
sheets of music out of his pocket, and sitting down on the bench
began to study them, occasionally beating out a rhythm on his
knee. Lupo stood in the middle of the room, the picture of guilt
looking about him like a mouse in a barrel.

"Seat yourself, friend," suggested Eduardo, "and abate the
knocking of your knees. A babe would suspect you of illegal
dealings at the moment."

Obediently Lupo sat on the very edge of the bench, but almost immediately leaped up again and flung himself upon a stray pamphlet, lurking half under the locked door. He stood then, his eyes popping out of his head and waving the paper frantically. Eduardo swore with his hand inside his coat and then thrust a cigarillo into his colleague's open mouth. Quickly he struck a match, set the pamphlet alight and applied the flame to the cigarillo, just as the door from the orchestra pit creaked open to admit a dapper young man.

Eduardo, though evidently possessed of great presence of mind, might have been better advised to discover whether Lupo shared his habit of smoking. The violinist drew in a lungful of the pungent smoke and promptly began to choke and splutter, till his eyes streamed and his face became purple with distress. In fact, if the newcomer had not, like all newcomers to that orchestra room, nearly brained himself on the lintel of the low room he would have been bound to wonder at such a scene. As it was, he was in no condition to notice anything but constellations reeling in their courses until Eduardo, clucking sympathetically, had steered him to a seat on the bench and anxiously examined the dark curly hair for signs of blood. By that time Lupo had recovered and was sitting damp-eyed and exhausted, eyeing the smouldering cigarillo as if it were an unexploded petard.

Finding nothing but an accumulation of pomade and an incipient lump, Eduardo stood back and wiped his fingers on a huge red silk handkerchief.

"Lupo, fetch wine! Poor youngster ... he has knocked his brains into a porridge."

The violinist thankfully handed over the cigarillo, accepted a few soldi in exchange, and scuttled through a third door which gave on to the passage leading to the stage door and the dressing rooms. The newcomer tried to get up but was pressed back on to the bench.

"My viola ..." he croaked, "my instrument ..."

"It is here! Behold!" comforted Eduardo and placed a battered case at his feet together with a curly-brimmed hat.

"I am Cesare Galeffi," declared the newcomer, "viola ..."

"Behold!" said Eduardo joyfully and shook him by the hand. "We have sore need of a viola but Signor Carettoni, he has declared that another instrument will bring him to ruin . . . I am Eduardo Torcellano, 'cello . . ."

"Ah," said the young man and sat up rather gingerly, his hand on the top of his head, as if he were afraid that the top of his skull might fall open, "I have a letter . . . one Signor Antonio Rioba has told me to enquire for you."

"Aha!" Eduardo responded as vibrantly as his own 'cello and he kissed the young Cesare enthusiastically upon both cheeks. "You are no doubt of our brotherhood, no?"

"From Milano," said Cesare and pulled out a letter, "I am of the Society of Young Carbonari there and I am sent to help in the struggle against the oppressor. I have some names . . . the Signor of the letter tells me you will know them."

"This very night you will come with me! At the café where I play after the opera they all come, the patriots. They know Papa Eduardo will have something for them."

He winked and laid his forefinger along his nose.

"Behold!"

He flung open the lid of the 'cello case and revealed the tightly packed pamphlets. Cesare pulled one out and read a pithy, if somewhat smudged, condemnation of those turpitudinous Venetians, who showed their weak-kneed toleration of the hatred Austrian usurper, by being present in the Piazza at the time when the bands of those mercenary hirelings of the forces of oppression, played the trumpery music of the conqueror . . . and much more in the same strain. Cesare nodded approval and put it back.

"These are our part in the affair," explained Eduardo, knocking upon the inner door in a significant way so that the thumping of the press resumed, "these, and newspapers giving news that the Austrians keep from us and posters which the young men paste upon the walls at dead of night . . . behold! Here they are set and printed . . ."

He spread out his plump hand stained with nicotine and printers' ink.

"In necessity I can set a little as you see but our task is to be couriers."

He sat down beside Cesare.

"You must understand that most of the orchestra play for the customers in cafés. The pay here is miserable beyond description ... not sufficient to keep alive a mouse of miniscule appetites. The Comitato Veneto..."

Cesare looked his enquiry.

"Your Signor Antonio Rioba..." explained Eduardo, "he is really a group of men bound to rid this city of the Austrian by any means in their power. Now the good Signor... he has provided some of us with another instrument which we keep in the cafés so that when we leave here we carry these..."

He indicated the pamphlet-packed cases.

"... while our own instruments lie safe in there with the press and the paper."

"And in the cafés?"

"The pamphlets are collected during the evening and the next day they appear on chairs and tables ... between the leaves of books, under plates, in folded napkins, under the hood of a gondola ... in a man's pocket, in his wife's sunshade..."

Lupo scuttled back into the room clutching two half-opened bottles of red wine. Eduardo rose and took one of them.

"Lupo, my friend, the stranger is of our number ... embrace him!"

Lupo compromised with a handshake and a timid smile.

"And in what way do you further the cause?" he enquired.

"I am come to enlist the youth of the city," declared Cesare, "only through the young will come the regeneration so needed in this ancient city..."

He did not observe the somewhat piqued expression on the faces ... the middle-aged faces ... of his two new acquaintances.

"From youth," he continued, "will come the fire and the energy we need to throw off the yoke. What is needed is action! I am here to promote that action. I bring aid and advice from Free Italy and we will begin to harass the usurper till he wishes he had never set foot here."

"To Free Italy!" interpolated Eduardo who had pulled out the cork with his teeth. "May Venice soon be one with her!"

"Amen . . . death to the Austrian!"

Lupo took his turn at the bottle with the air of a blood-thirsty mouse. Cesare shrugged hugely and then winced as the movement hurt his head.

"As to that matter," he said and twisted his face into a sneer, "no doubt it can be arranged . . . at last. When Youth is stirred into action then Freedom will be in sight!"

He took the bottle and drank to this sentiment, but found the raw red stuff a little overpowering and choked, a circumstance which gave the other two patriots a certain satisfaction. Lupo deftly removed the bottle and drank again.

"Tell me," asked Cesare, "does our friend Carettoni know of these . . . activities?"

He gestured at the door and the pamphlets in a manner which held a touch of contempt.

Eduardo shrugged.

"He knows and he knows not."

"The press?"

Once more the 'cellist put his finger to his nose.

"A man of influence has decided he no longer wishes to live in an occupied city . . . there are many of these, you understand, their absence is part of the Dimostrazione against the Austrian . . . and so he gives up his Palazzo and must store his possessions against the coming of freedom. Carettoni obliges him with a storeroom, at a price of course, and if the dirty Tedeschi search the theatre and find a press who so surprised as Carettoni, who? Meanwhile the man of influence is safe in Milano."

"Understood," Cesare nodded.

"And then another man of influence, one who has *not* left the city, he has developed an interest of the heart in the company, which brings him here nearly every day. And if his pockets contain the writings of the Comitato Veneto for that press the good Signor Carettoni is not to know . . . nor is La Fiorella as long as his other pockets contain flowers and trinkets for her."

Unexpectedly Lupo sighed.

"Ah," he exclaimed, "such eyes, such a blue like the robe of the Virgin, and such a figure as she has the little English one."

He kissed his fingers.

"And such a disaster of a voice . . ." returned Eduardo uncharacteristically acid, "how she came by this engagement is a mystery not wholly beyond divination."

He drank again.

"Signor del Doria has a rival in that quarter," said Lupo his eyes on the rapidly falling level in the bottle.

Eduardo made a wide gesture of dislike and contempt.

"A filthy little Tedescho . . . that is no rival."

Lupo shook his head.

"Tedescho maybe, but you forget . . . La Fiorella is not Venetian, she is English. She hasn't our detestation of the Austrian. And they are all great snobs these English and he is the son of a Count!"

Eduardo's face reddened.

"Son of an Austrian count! Son of a dunghill cock! What is a Tedescho Graf to a noble of Venice?"

"There are some things she might consider," persisted Lupo taking his chance with the bottle.

"What for example?" demanded Eduardo.

"Marriage, for example."

"Marriage!"

Eduardo exploded into laughter.

"Who would marry that one?"

"Von Fuschl is young, foolish and tail over top in love," said Lupo. "Me, I would not bet upon his chances of escaping matrimony. And . . ."

He raised the empty bottle and pointed the neck of it at Eduardo.

"I know of one not a league from here who would propose marriage to her sister . . . if he could find a stool to stand upon."

Eduardo glowered and Cesare looked bewildered.

"The sister of La Fiorella, she is two metres high and built like the goddesses of old," explained Lupo, "and Eduardo has conceived a passion for her."

14

"She is a very different person," snapped Eduardo, "she resembles her sister in no particular. And she is at least a musician . . . as one can hear."

He paused and pointed upwards to the boards of the stage.

"She plays the pianoforte for the répétition," explained Lupo, "and she copies the musical parts for the orchestra . . ."

The door to the corridor was flung open and a large red-faced man came in carrying a trumpet. He was clearly more than a little drunk and bursting with news.

"La Fiorella . . ." he began, "she entertains the Tedesco in her dressing room."

"So that is news!" said Lupo scornfully.

The trumpet-player's eye lighted on the unbroached wine-bottle and he swooped upon it.

"But this *is* news, I promise you . . ."

He pulled out the loosened cork with his teeth and drank deeply until Eduardo pulled it away.

"What is news?" he demanded.

"The walls of those dressing rooms they are like paper. You can hear the scratching of the mice next door. I was sharing a bottle with Mario in his room . . ."

"The work of a moment!" commented Eduardo bitterly, disposing of what remained in his bottle.

"Mario is the principal tenor," explained Lupo. "He sings best when he is drunk."

"Which is to say less badly than when he is sober," added Eduardo.

"I heard them arguing, the Tedesco and La Fiorella. He said she was a faithless, heartless cocotte . . ."

"So what is news?" said Lupo and sighed.

". . . and she said that he was a foolish, jealous creature and that she would never play him false. And then he shouted that she lied in her teeth and she was encouraging the attentions of del Doria . . ."

Eduardo nodded significantly at Cesare.

". . . for behold! there lay his gift upon her table! It is her name day today . . . or so she says."

15

"She had a name day six months ago," commented Eduardo, "and another four months before that..."

"And von Fuschl shouted at her," the trumpet player went on, "he shouted, 'Make your choice, faithless one! For me, I will not be driven in a pair-harness... if you are to be mine you will be mine alone. If you value my love, wear my gift tonight. Unless it is on your breast when you enter I will never see you again. And if you wear that trumpery I will kill you!' With these ears I heard him. And then he slammed the door so that all the rooms shook and went away."

"And what is his gift?" asked Cesare.

"Diamonds," said the trumpeter. "A necklace of diamonds, very fine and worth a mint of money. And del Doria has sent a pendent of sapphires and pearls... she ran after the Tedescho down the corridor to soothe him you understand, and I peeped in to see."

"So... if La Fiorella wears diamonds tonight del Doria can come here no longer," concluded Eduardo. "This could make certain difficulties..."

When the répétition was over and the pamphlets all stowed, he went in search of the pianist and insisted that she join him in a dish of baccala.

"... for I must speak with you... it is imperative."

What he had to ask was that she try to persuade her sister to reject von Fuschl's offer. Mary simply smiled placidly upon his agitation. Eduardo shook his head at her unconcern and examined another aspect of the affair.

"Only consider, Meess Porretusa..."

Porteous was a name which did not adapt easily to Italian tongues.

"... it will not be good for the theatre if the diva should become known as an Austriaca... and the dear Lord knows that business is sufficiently bad..."

Venice deplored the Austrian reconquest of 1849 by a kind of perpetual public mourning from which attendances at public entertainment suffered severely.

"Signor Eduardo," said Mary gently, "Flora... La Fiorella

... may be my sister, but please disabuse yourself of the notion that I can influence her in any way, for I cannot."

Eduardo sighed.

"You must realise that there is more at stake than a few boxes more or less. It is a question of ..."

Mary interrupted him.

"I know what's at stake in this case ..."

She laid a delicate emphasis on the last word and laughed at his dismay.

"It's to be hoped that the Austrians are as unsuccessful in discovering conspiracy as you are in concealing it. But I would not worry too much, my friend. Flora knows very well on which side her bread is buttered ... and she gets a percentage of the takings."

Eduardo's brow cleared and he addressed himself to the salt cod on his plate with more appetite.

The orchestra was making those confused and exciting discords which herald the advent of the conductor. The audience in the Teatro Benedetto was settling down to the evening's entertainment. It was a curiously subdued assembly. The pit was thronged with soberly dressed Venetians, shopkeepers and craftsmen for the most part, bargaining for places on the benches round the walls or for the stools hired out in the pit. The rows of chairs near the orchestra remained empty. In the first and second tiers the wealthier members of society were already seated in the very back of their boxes, wearing sad-coloured clothes and very little jewellery.

In the orchestra pit Eduardo leaned over to Cesare who was looking about him in a somewhat daunted fashion.

"I did warn you," he said, "this isn't Milano. Ours isn't a brilliant society. The Austrian occupation's to blame because the Dimostrazione against it keeps all the best people away. And I warn you, those who do come pretend not to enjoy themselves."

Cesare looked at him in dismay.

17

"There won't be any cheers or bravos . . . just a little clapping."

Eduardo drew his bow over the strings and made a melancholy thrumming sound.

"Mind," he remarked, "we haven't had a bomb in the theatre for some time now."

A hint of animation came into Cesare's expression.

"Bombs, eh?" he murmured.

Eduardo jerked his bow at a commotion round the entrance to the pit.

"Here they come . . . the sons of whores." he remarked.

A lively crowd of young men in white and gold uniforms began to push their way through the people standing in the pit. Some had colourful young women hanging on their arms. They spread out along the rows of gilt chairs at the front, laughing loudly and shouting to one another in German. Cesare looked at them with concentrated dislike.

"Noisy crew, they are."

"The Austrian officers from the garrison," explained Eduardo, "and the one sitting right behind the conductor's podium is Herr Kapitan Steiger von Fuschl."

The Herr Kapitan was a not unimpressive figure. Of medium height he radiated an aura of energy and virility like a pony stallion.

"Is del Doria here?" asked Cesare looking about.

Eduardo shook his head.

"He never attends the actual performance. The nobles don't, you know . . . or if they do it's incognito. But don't worry, there'll be plenty to tell him if La Fiorella chooses to wear diamonds . . . the story's all over Venice."

Cesare was still looking around him, staring at the rapidly filling gallery and the crowd milling about in the pit behind the gilt chairs. From the back of every box there glimmered the vague shape of faces.

"I understood that you commonly had poor houses," he observed, "this doesn't look poor to me. In fact I would say you hadn't a place to spare."

Eduardo looked up from his instrument and considered the unusual size of the audience and for the first time another aspect of the situation occurred to him. He groaned a little apprehensively.

"Body of Bacchus. I said it myself... the story's all over Venice! The good saints prevail upon the little bitch to wear the pendent..."

At this point the répétiteur emerged from the orchestra room, acknowledged the non-existent applause, tapped with his baton on the stand, and the meagre orchestra played a ragged chord and dashed with much verve and little accuracy into the overture. Of this the audience took no notice whatsoever, waiting to finish their conversations until the curtain went up. The lights in the auditorium were put out and the curtain rose on a somewhat shabby set.

Behind the stage La Fiorella put the finishing touches to her make-up, adorned her hair with two rather grubby feathers and dusted her superb shoulders with powder. The reflection in the glass appeared to satisfy her so she rose, and the waiting dresser with a kind of casual skill flung the overdress over her head without touching feathers, hair or face. It was laced, hooked and settled over the panniers and under the stomacher. The dresser vanished wordlessly to perform the same service for the contralto next door, who was playing the Queen in the second Act. La Fiorella returned to her dressing table and considered the two leather cases which lay side by side in a sordid muddle of greasepaint, powder, hairpins, pomade and haircombings. She opened both of them. Her pretty, slightly petulant face gave no sign of the argument she was conducting between her senses and her common sense.

First she considered the diamonds. A woman of intelligence should recognise the advantages of secure wealth; del Doria's fortune, large as it was, could vanish at the whim of an occupying power. Von Fuschl was very much *épris*; 'silly about me' was how she phrased it to herself. Such 'silliness' would make him more susceptible to... well... to pressure. Flora Jane

Porteous on the threshold of the thirties and in a notoriously precarious profession, would dearly like the security of a wedding ring and Steiger von Fuschl was just obtuse enough and just enamoured enough to make this ring a possibility. Pappi and Mutti in Vienna would very much dislike the idea but Steiger was unlikely to succumb to parental pressure (his allowance was secured). This being the case, she would in time become the Gräfin von Fuschl, or else she would be handsomely compensated for her broken heart by Pappi and Mutti. It was a pleasantly profitable prospect either way.

She picked the pendent out of its case and turned the sapphires under the candles till they flashed blue. Todaro was so much more ... her very bones melted when he touched her. What was more to the point, he was wealthy and there were no parents alive to complicate matters; he had control of his whole fortune too, unlike Steiger whose allowance was barely adequate for his (admittedly exacting) requirements.

La Fiorella was shrewd enough to realise, however, that her Todaro was much, much less *épris* than Steiger. In fact, occasionally, she wondered ... there had been opportunities which he had unaccountably ignored, appointments he had missed. The arrival of the pendent, though she would not have admitted this to anyone but herself, had been a welcome surprise. Her chances of persuading del Doria into matrimony would appear slim. A liaison with him might be sweet but it would certainly be short (on current form) and likely to be ended at his whim, not hers. Furthermore, del Doria was fixed in Venice by his boring politics and Venice these days was indubitably the dreariest town in all Italy, whereas Steiger was to be posted to brilliant Vienna where La Fiorella, the third-rate soprano, could blossom into somebody much more exotic. Her mind revolved lovingly about a notion of waltzes, chandeliers and uniforms. She laid the pendent back on its velvet tray and lifted the diamonds : they were, she knew, fairly good stones (a visit to a jeweller had been a sensible precaution), but the setting was ugly, old-fashioned and clumsy. The first thing she would do in Vienna would be to have them reset, heirlooms or no heirlooms. She clasped the necklace round her perfect throat and admired the effect. With a firm and final gesture she clicked shut the lid of the pendent box.

A boy thumped on her door and shouted,

"Cinque! Cinque, Signorina!"

She picked up a huge fan sewn with brilliants and swept along the passage to the stage entrance.

On stage, hero and heroine were pledging deathless fidelity interminably prolonged. There was a patter of polite applause skilfully milked by the tenor and she was on, greeted by a profound hush as the well-informed audience scanned her bosom. They were frustrated at first by the fan over which she ogled the hero. The arpeggios which heralded her flirtatious assault upon his long-vaunted fidelity rattled out of the orchestra pit; she lowered the fan and drew in a breath but before she could release it in her first notes there was a noise in the gloom beyond the floats. It was an ominous, hostile noise which resolved itself into a chanting of "Diamanti! Diamanti!"

Startled she peered into the darkness and was greeted by a hissing, "A abbasso Austriacanti! A abbasso Austriacanti!" This was countered by another kind of hissing and shushing as the occupants of the boxes demanded silence. They were not to have it. A voice high up in the gallery yelled shrilly.

"Viva Sior Antonio Rioba!"

To which the audience responded with a full-throated cheer and more "A abbasso Austriacanti!"

Cesare dropped his viola to his lap and turned to Eduardo.

"What in the name of Jupiter is all this about?"

Eduardo was gathering his music up into a sheaf.

"They want to cut the throats of Austrian-lovers," he explained rather unnecessarily, because the audience was now roaring out its desire to have these undesirables subjected to a number of unpleasant fates.

"And who *is* this Sior Antonio?"

"Well, it is a name they give to a statue near the old Ghetto, but they use it to mean the resistance to the Austrians, it's a sort of nom de guerre..."

His voice was drowned in the roar of the crowd who had now begun to shout, "A abbasso la puttana Austriaca!"

La Fiorella who, like Marie Antoinette, did not relish being called an Austrian whore, had dropped all attempts to continue her role and was shouting abuse at her abusers, when there was a splat and a splash on the stage beside her, and the tenor spluttered out an oath as a tomato hit him amidships on his canary-coloured breeches. The yells from the gallery and the pit became more confused and there were peremptory shouts for 'Lights!' from the seats near the orchestra. Another tomato hit La Fiorella on the chest and dribbled down into her fichu, dimming the diamonds. Rotten fruit in suspiciously large quantities now began to shower on to the stage mingled with soldi, which were hurled with stinging force as if their throwers were determined to get their money's worth. La Fiorella, struck by a stinking onion, put her hands on her hips and shrieked at the audience like an angry cat, calling them sons of dogs and figures of pigs in true Venetian style. To such compliments the audience replied in the coarsest terms, mostly incomprehensible to anyone born outside Venice; possibly suspecting that these might be lost upon their victim, they backed them up with a further hail of missiles. La Fiorella, stung painfully upon the mouth by an apple, put her hands to her face and fled, sobbing with anger and fear, just as the lights were lit in the auditorium.

They revealed a scene of unholy confusion. In the recess under the first tier of boxes, the occupants of the pit were fighting and shouting. There appeared to be several schools of thought: those who disapproved of La Fiorella and her choice; those who disapproved of her choice but approved of La Fiorella; those who knew nothing of what was afoot and wanted to hear the opera for which they had paid to come in; those who approved of Tedeschi-baiting, whatever the excuse; and finally there was the inevitable element who were prepared to enjoy any kind of a dust-up. The result of these conflicting views was a mêlée of a kind unknown in the Benedetto since an unpaid company walked out on the management just before the performance was due to start.

The genteel occupants of the boxes were hastily gathering up their cloaks and wraps, and escorting their twittering women-folk to the exits. The white-uniformed Austrians near the orchestra, hemmed in by the fighters, bunched together and glared like angry cattle. The orchestra, which had suffered from the bombardment, scuttled into the orchestra room under a fresh hail of missiles and Eduardo locked the door. Unfortunately not all the members of the orchestra had reached safety : the bass-viol player, unwilling to abandon his unwieldy instrument had been left behind and locked out together with the trumpet-player who had been asleep when the trouble began and slept on in the belief that they were presenting the *Fliegende Holländer*. Between them they could not make themselves understood in the orchestra room where their hammerings were thought to be the harbingers of the riot. A shower of rotten tomatoes decided them to beat a retreat another way, so they hoisted the bass-viol up on to the stage and began in undignified style to hoist themselves up after it, under a hail of missiles from the gallery, where the steepness of the rake inhibited the patrons from starting a rough-house like that in the pit. They were bombarding the Austrian officers with whatever came to hand . . . and it was a good deal. Their aim was erratic but the number and variety of the missiles more than made up for that.

The two musicians heaved themselves on to the empty stage and made for the wings, just in time to be obliterated by the dusty purple-plush folds of the curtain, which had been dropped precipitately by the assistant stage manager. He had seen the two scramble on to the stage and thought that they heralded an invasion from the auditorium. The last the howling and delighted audience saw of them was the trumpet-player's white-stockinged legs kicking feebly, as their owner fought his way through to the rear. From immediately below the stage box the manager erupted on to the stage, his grey hair standing frantic-ally on end, waving his arms like a spider in a basin. The noise drowned the remarks he passionately wished to make, and while the gallery was beginning to run out of ammunition, the patrons of the pit were breaking off the backs and legs of the benches round the walls to use as clubs. This sight made the manager fairly dance with fury.

Meanwhile the beleaguered Austrian officers had made a decision : ignoring the manager who was offering, albeit inaudibly, to let them out by the stage door, they formed a line across the floor of the pit and drew their swords, evidently intending to cut their way out.

The noise died down as the rioters observed the drawn swords, and the manager's protests, pleas and threats began to make themselves heard in the ugly hush. He implored the audience not to murder one another, or if they found the urge to do so irresistible (and it was clear that he found it understandable), he begged that they might do so outside his so-beautiful theatre.

There was no evidence that anyone was prepared to listen to his plea, but just at that dramatic moment there came an equally theatrical intervention. From the stage box on the prompt side there came a raucous and uproarious voice, its source a cloaked figure masked in the grim white maschera of the eighteenth century who stood in the shadow at the back of the box.

"Hey, friends ! Let pass our little Austrian guests ! The poor little fellows ... let them by !"

He gave vent to the high-pitched, warbling yell by which a gondolier demands passage. He spoke in the broadest Venetian dialect and was greeted with a roar of 'Sior Antonio ! Viva ! Viva !'

"Come along with you, sons of dogs !" roared 'Sior Antonio' "remember that Venetians are always hospitable to their guests ... even the unwelcome ones !"

There was a roar of laughter at that comment and the officers, whose heroic stance was by this time falling a trifle flat, scowled.

"Come now, come ! Put down those bits of firewood. Come, obstinate dogs ! Let the poor little creatures safe home to their Daddy Francis ! He doesn't know they're out without their nurse. Mind your manners now, my friends !"

The crowd stirred good-humouredly at this irreverent reference to the hated emperor, threw down its improvised weapons, and made a passage to the door with much mock ceremony. The Austrians sheathed their swords with a hiss and a thump and moved out with as much dignity as they could muster through the ironical bows and sarcastic compliments. Only von Fuschl lingered staring up at the shadowy figure in the box.

"You! You, whoever you are!" he called out, "you haven't heard the last of this, I promise you."

The cloaked figure laughed.

"I will have examples made for this!" shouted the Austrian, "The Emperor is not to be insulted in this way!"

"Content yourself with little triumphs, little man," returned the 'Sior' provocatively and slipped out of the door of the box.

Von Fuschl hesitated for a moment, his handsome face screwed into a scowl, and then he turned about, leaped on to the stage and ran into the wings, pushing the almost-apoplectic manager rudely out of his way.

"Who might the *deus ex machina* be?" asked Cesare rather breathlessly.

Those members of the orchestra whose cases contained the produce of the illicit press had decided that it would be only tactful to remove themselves and their contraband before the police came to investigate the evening's events. They felt tolerably certain that the opera would not be resumed. Eduardo and Cesare were heading for a café in the Campo Morosini, which was much frequented by the choicer spirits of the Italianissimi and going at a pace designed to put as much distance between themselves and the uproar as quickly as was possible.

"Sior Antonio?" puffed Eduardo. "It could have been any of the Comitato Veneto . . . but from the height I think it was del Doria."

"What I don't understand," confided Cesare as they dived under a sottoportega, "is why he should want to stop things. It was a promising situation . . . those officers could have been disposed of to a man!"

Eduardo stopped and put down the heavy 'cello case.

"My friend, you are a hot-headed fool. They would have died no doubt, but how many innocent souls with them? And how many more would vanish into the prisons? It was enough to humiliate them."

Cesare said nothing, but it was plain he thought very little of such a pusillanimous attitude.

When they arrived at the café it was to see in one corner a familiar figure, tall and well-built, his long legs stretched out before him and studying a newspaper. On the rickety table at his elbow a pile of coffee saucers pointed to the probability of his having occupied that chair since early evening. It was hard to imagine the raucous familiarities of 'Sior Antonio' emerging from that languid boulevardier. Del Doria acknowledged Eduardo's arrival with a nod at the chairs on the other side of the table. Another nod at the scurrying waiter brought forth the mechanical "Behold me!" and in a few minutes a tray with two cups of coffee.

"Well, Signor Eduardo, you are early tonight."

Eduardo seconded by Cesare poured forth the tale of the evening's disorders, a recital which lost nothing in the telling, and won more attention for Eduardo from the patrons of the café, than ever he could command with his 'cello. At the end . . .

"She must go with the Tedescho," cried Eduardo, "I am convinced of it!"

Del Doria sipped his coffee and nodded.

"It seems," he observed, "that I will need to cultivate a passion for a marionette. And why not . . . such charming and uncomplicated creatures as they are . . . I shall have to bring them into fashion, don't you think?"

From which it was to be understood that the next refuge for the illicit press would be the Marionette Theatre in the Calle di Ridotto.

Behind the stage at the Benedetto the drama was not yet over. La Fiorella had barricaded her door and was trembling behind it, expecting that it was to be trampled down at any moment by a ravening mob. When von Fuschl, having given up his search for the 'Sior', shoved his way through the milling and apprehensive chorus, and hammered upon the panels, she squealed with terror and implored him to go away. With understandable irritation he bellowed out his claim to her consideration, but as she was crouched in the far corner with her hands over her ears and her eyes tightly shut it had little effect. This did not incommode her hero for long. The dressing rooms at the Benedetto were no more than cubicles with boarded partitions in between, and the partitions were no higher than would preserve the modesty of the occupants. Von Fuschl being both ardent and athletic jumped for the top of the partition and hauled himself over. La Fiorella peering timorously from her ambush by the dressing table, recognised her cavalier's legs before he had time to regain his balance, and hurled herself at him. They collapsed in an undignified tangle against the dusty curtain which protected La Fiorella's costumes. In her previous agitation she had omitted to remove the remains of a squashed tomato from her corsage, and her lover emerged from this embrace with a red stain on the breast of his white uniform, which was later to cause his soldier servant a deal of bother. This circumstance tended to distract his attention during the interview which followed, for he was nice in his notions of dress.

La Fiorella, in her fluent if somewhat inaccurate Italian, tearfully implored him to take her away from this awful place and these savage people; if he loved her, she wept, he would not expect her to endure the insults of the unwashed on his account. Von Fuschl, scrubbing at the stain with his handkerchief, responded rather bad-temperedly that this was exactly what he had been wanting to do for some time. As far as he was concerned, he frowned at the stain, it could not be too soon. At this La Fiorella launched herself at him again but he held her off rather ungallantly with one hand.

"For any favour, Fifi, rid yourself of *that*!" he demanded, indicating the squashed remains lingering messily among the laces at her bosom.

His beloved gave a squeak of dismay and made for the basin

and ewer, where she removed it and some other more obvious traces of her encounter with the opera-lovers of Venice.

"My leave begins tomorrow," said von Fuschl giving up the stain as a bad job, "I had thought that if you wanted we could travel to Vienna together in a day or two — give you time to make your arrangements — buy a hat and some fripperies, eh?"

But even such a prospect as that could not reconcile La Fiorella to any delay.

"I won't stay here another hour to be jeered at in the street and called horrid names!" she declared, "I won't...I'd rather die. If I'm to go with you at all you must take me tonight."

She wept over the sponge and the ewer.

"Calm yourself, my love," von Fuschl begged, "it can be arranged. I will bring a gondola to the Calle di Fuseri an hour after midnight and we can take the morning train to Mestre. From there we can be in Vienna in two days. Come, gather up your traps and let's go ..."

Once more La Fiorella flung herself upon him and this time he welcomed her with a prolonged embrace. It was, at length, interrupted by a thunderous demand for entry from the manager, who had had time to survey the damage to his beloved theatre and now wanted to put the blame where it belonged. The lovers parted unhurriedly and von Fuschl dismantled the barricade of chairs and trunks. When the door was unlocked it revealed Signor Carettoni, his hair on end, his stock awry and his eyes flashing with fury.

"You! You and your amours!" he exploded, "You have destroyed my so-beautiful theatre! You have cost me untold hundreds of lire! My plaster it is ruined, my chairs they are broken, my lamps they are smashed, my paint it will have to be cleaned from roof to cellar, my musicians are injured, their instruments matchwood, my singers ..."

He cast his eyes up to heaven to witness his agonies.

"... my singers will never be the same ..."

He pointed dramatically at La Fiorella.

"All this on account of your petty, sordid, little intrigue ... you have destroyed me!"

La Fiorella who had wilted a little before the initial onslaught now drew herself up and looked at him loftily in the manner of the Queen in the third act.

"That being the case," she declared in a ringing head voice, also used in the third act, "you will, no doubt welcome the news of my departure. I will not linger for a single unnecessary moment where I am not appreciated. I am going, going NOW!"

With a grand gesture she plucked her swansdown-trimmed cloak from the rickety sofa.

"Come Steiger..."

Von Fuschl bowed and held out his arm and they advanced upon the manager. It was plain to see that Signor Carettoni had reached boiling point. His face was purple and he spluttered incoherently.

"Tomorrow!" he succeeded in spitting out, barring their way, "tomorrow we give *Elisir d'Amore*... who will sing your role?"

La Fiorella clasped her cloak beneath her chin and tossed her head, a gesture a trifle spoiled by the circumstance of one of her feathers being broken across.

"I neither know nor care," she declared. "I will not stay for another minute in this... this bear-pit!"

"Bear-pit!" screamed Carettoni, "Bear-pit!"

"The behaviour tonight was that of the gutter!" La Fiorella informed him, "why should I stay to suffer insult!"

"Bear-pit!" repeated Carettoni, with whom this epithet seemed to rankle. "It is by far the best theatre that you will ever know! You... you with your pretty little face and your pretty little voice! Pshaw! I can find ten singers better than you in any whorehouse in Venice!"

"You may start by considering your own household," La Fiorella advised him, "you may find a number of such singers there!"

At this insult Carettoni could express his feelings only by snapping his fingers repeatedly under La Fiorella's nose. Von Fuschl, whose Italian was of that pedestrian nature to be expected of a member of the occupying power, and thus of no assistance to him in following a conversation of such a technical

29

and idiomatic description, decided it was time he took a hand in the proceedings. He drew his sword and placed the tip just above the fourth button of the manager's satin waistcoat.

"Figure of a pig," he observed (for he knew that much Italian), "let us pass if you value your licence. It is plain after what happened tonight that your theatre is a hotbed of sedition. I will represent to my seniors that it is time and high time it was closed down."

He spoke fluently but as an Englishman might speak French, without concession to accent or inflection : this did not prevent the manager from understanding him very clearly. Even if he had mistaken the meaning, a jab from the sword was enough to remind him who was the occupying power. Fulminating sulphurously under his breath, Carettoni stood aside to let von Fuschl usher his inamorata through the door. As he did so the swansdown-trimmed cloak floated back to reveal that she had not, in the press of events, found time to change out of her costume. The manager emitted a sound like an agitated train whistle and pursued the pair along the corridor.

"Thieves! Robbers! Banditti!" he apostrophised them, "What of my so-beautiful costume?"

La Fiorella tried to ensure that her last exit from the Benedetto was dramatically telling. She stopped under the lamp which flickered above the stage entrance, turned like a ship in a seaway and flung open her cloak.

"Behold your so-beautiful costume!" she cried. "This sordid, stained and filthy rag will be returned to you in the morning by one who will remove my own possessions. The blemishes caused by the kind attentions of your bestial patrons are no concern of mine!"

She swept the cloak shut and turned her shoulder on the manager. Von Fuschl, who was beginning to have enough of drama, again offered his arm; but Carettoni had got his second wind and was set upon having the last word.

"It hurts me to the heart!" he shouted after them, his hand upon that expanse of grubby satin which concealed it. "It hurts me beyond description that my Venetians should thus express their opinion of your morals !"

He paused and drew breath.

"What concern was it of theirs that you should have the morals of an alley cat? If they had but bombarded you because you sing like one !"

2

"... Farewell, without a Grudge!"

La Bohème: PUCCINI

LA FIORELLA, BIDDING A passionate if temporary, farewell to her cavalier at the steps by the bridge, was slightly pained by his unromantic request that she bring with her all the money she had.

"I'll borrow what I can," he assured her, "but this sudden departure prevents my visiting my bankers and Vienna is a long way from here—"

She agreed to this.

"In an hour then, beloved," said von Fuschl, "and ..."

He handed her up the steps to the fondamente.

"... for once in your existence, my sweet bird, be punctual."

The key to the lodgings was not difficult to find being nearly nine inches long and this was as well for the Calle was ill-lit. She closed the door as softly as she could and crept upstairs to the two rooms on the second floor which she shared with her sister. In the larger of the two she found a candle guttering low and from it lit a fresh one, which she set on the table lurking under a heavy plush cover. From the depths of the armoire in the corner, she dragged a shabby carpet-bag and a leather portemanteau, both of which she set open. Then, shading the flame with her hand, she took the light into the other room. The curtains of the vast four-poster bed which she shared with her sister Mary, were drawn but La Fiorella put the candle down behind a chair, so that the light would not fall on the curtains. By this uncertain illumination she opened the drawers of the chest which contained her clothes and removed the contents.

Back in the other room she stuffed them higgledy-piggledy

into the bags and when they were full and strapped shut, she lugged them downstairs one at a time. Next, she took off the stained costume, dropping it on the floor, and with a speed and ease which would have astonished the over-worked dresser at the Benedetto, put on the three skirts and several petticoats for which the portemanteau had not afforded space. This done she brought out a bonnet-box bearing the name of an exclusive milliner in the Calle della Ascensione and went back into the bedroom where, from a small drawer in the dressing-table, she removed several leather cases and lastly a plump purse. The cases she bestowed among the silver paper which protected the elegant hat, and the purse was put in a safer place down the front of her bodice. Next she took the leather case containing the rejected sapphire pendent from her reticule. Heightened emotions at the Benedetto had not served to make her forget such a trifle. She raised the lid and regarded its graceful workmanship with regret, a regret tempered as always with common sense. Steiger would never permit her to wear it, in fact he would probably hurl it into the canal if he found it. Furthermore, it made it possible to meet an awkward obligation in a manner at once generous and, in the circumstances, economical. There was an inkstand on the table and some sheets of paper. La Fiorella retrieved the candle and began to write a letter, looking up in a slightly hunted fashion when the church clock of San Luca struck the quarter. When she had scrawled a few lines, she folded the sheets and tried to fit it into the pendent case, but it was too thick to permit the lid to close, so she removed the velvet-covered tray on which the jewel lay and put the letter into the space underneath. With it she placed an old-fashioned emerald signet ring she had removed from one of the jewel-cases. Carefully she replaced the tray and snapped the lid shut. That done she glanced at the clock on the chest and gave a squeak of dismay. On the shabby sofa she had left a furlined cloak, a fur muff and a high-crowned hat which she put on quickly. With the jewel-box in her hand, she tip-toed into the bedroom and laid it on the dressing-table. She turned about, shading the candle with her hand and then jumped so that she nearly dropped it.

33

"And just what are you up to, Flora?" enquired Mary who was sitting on the edge of the bed taking in the scene; she considered the furlined cloak and the hat, "And where are you going?"

"Oh, Lor'," exclaimed the runaway ruefully.

Under Mary's calm and somewhat amused gaze, she gave a confused account of the evening's events at the Benedetto and the decision to leave immediately.

"I did write you a letter," she explained, "you see, Mary, I need the money : I must have something of my own . . . just in case . . ."

Mary made no comment.

"You *must* see that," said La Fiorella though she sounded less than convinced herself, "But I haven't forgotten you, Mary, I promise."

She flourished the pendent-case.

"It's that pendent Todaro sent me. It's valuable . . . about a thousand lire, the jeweller said . . ."

Mary laughed and her sister looked injured.

"I'm sure I don't know what you find so funny . . ."

Mary laughed more than ever and La Fiorella abandoned the mystery with a shrug and went back to business.

"You can sell it and get enough to buy a passage home . . . more than enough."

Mary said nothing.

"For heaven's sake, say something," demanded her sister irritably, "it's my money after all! I made every penny of it."

"I know," said Mary calmly and rose to put on her dressing-gown.

"I'll write when I'm married and you can come and stay and . . ."

"Oh," said Mary, "so you're to be married?"

"Of course," replied La Fiorella crossly.

"Does the gallant captain know this?"

La Fiorella slapped the case down on to the dressing table and glared angrily up at her sister.

"I was going to say that we could try to find you a husband

34

but how we could do that outside a freak show I do not know . . ."

Mary smiled.

"Indeed, nor do I. Please don't trouble yourself, Flora, I'm not sure I want a husband of your finding."

La Fiorella flounced to the door, the draught she created almost extinguishing the candle.

"I am late," she announced.

"And will the gallant captain not wait for you?"

"Oh, he will," La Fiorella assured her, "but the Mestre train will not."

"Goodbye then . . . and good luck."

Mary made no move towards her sister but stayed beside the bed, her shadow swaying fantastically on the wall behind her. La Fiorella hesitated.

"I'll write . . ." she said, "where will you go?"

"I hardly know," replied Mary, "but I'll leave an address with the theatre. Write there."

La Fiorella looked doubtful, but before she could explain that the current climate at the theatre might not be conducive to the forwarding of letters, she was reminded of another matter.

"Oh, Mary . . . there's my costume. I said it would be returned. Would you? It's in the next room. And there are some things of mine in the dressing room."

"Oh, very well," said Mary, "I'll tidy up after you for the last time. For his own sake I hope the gallant captain can afford a maid for you."

"I do wish you wouldn't call Steiger that. It makes him sound . . . oh, I don't know . . ."

"*I* know," said Mary with a note of relish.

Her sister hunched an impatient shoulder and turned away.

"Flora . . ."

Mary's voice had changed, lost its teasing note.

"Flora, I don't suppose it would serve any useful purpose to suggest that this isn't very wise . . . or very admirable . . ."

"I'm the best judge of what is wise for me," said La Fiorella.

". . . aren't you being rather foolish?"

"I'd be a lot more foolish to turn him down," said her sister bluntly, "I haven't much voice, you know that ... it's only my looks which have got me this far. I'll never go further."

Mary said nothing.

"In a year or two they'll start to fade, my looks ... and then what?"

Again Flora got no answer.

"You can fend for yourself, Mary. You can play the pianoforte, copy music, teach drawing and singing ... I can't."

"Your talents are a little different," agreed Mary and Flora laughed ruefully.

"That being the case, I must make best use of them while I can. I have to go, Mary. He'll be waiting. I'll write, I promise, and if you're in any sort of difficulty I'll send you more money. But that ..."

She nodded in the direction of the case on the dressing table.

"... that'll fetch plenty to get you home. Goodbye."

She went. Mary heard her running down the stairs and went to the window where she could see her sister met by a cloaked and impatient figure. Her last view of the precious pair was under the light on the bridge where they were boarding a gondola, von Fuschl loaded with baggage in a manner most damaging to his dignity. Mary smiled and went back to the pillaged dressing table. The silver brushes, the embossed mirrors, silver boxes, all had gone. Only the blue leather case lay there among an abandoned litter of hairpins and silver paper. Mary looked down at it for a second, frowning, then she shrugged and went back to bed.

Morning in the Calle di Fuseri began as it usually did. Signora Matteo, who kept the lodging house, emerged from the tiny bedroom on the ground floor, put on her morning wrapper and a splendid beribboned cap to conceal her curl-papers, and proceeded to light a charcoal brazier and prepare coffee while Francesca the maid went scurrying along to the Campo San Luca in search of new bread. Grunts and wheezings from the bedroom announced the imminent uprising of Signor Matteo.

His wife was fanning away at the brazier to quicken the coals, when Mary knocked on the door and came in as one sure of a welcome. The Signora with an eloquent gesture of her unengaged hand showered matutinal blessings upon her lodger and nodded to a chair.

"I can be but a tiny moment . . . Francesca will return like a flash of lightning . . . your sister need wait no longer than that!"

She held up her hand with thumb and forefinger measuring on infinitesimal degree.

"I came down to tell you, Signora," said Mary calmly, "my sister is no longer here. She left suddenly last night."

The Signora flashed a significant, darkling look across the room at her guest.

"So!" she commented portentously.

"And I, Signora, must leave also. And soon. Today, I fear."

"You return, without doubt, to Inghilterra?"

"No, Signora. I remain in Venice."

A final flourish of the fan and the coffee was ready. The Signora poured it neat-handedly, filling two vast bowls for herself and the Signor and an elegant porcelain cup for Mary. As the last drop was poured, Francesca came panting in bringing with her the scent of hot bread. The Matteo household addressed itself to breakfast.

"So!" exclaimed the Signora, rather crumbily. "You stay in Venice and yet you are to leave us. Is it that you can no longer endure our company?"

Her superb eyebrows met above her nose, which was more Roman than Venetian, in a terrifying frown.

"No, Signora," said Mary serenely, "merely that I can no longer afford to enjoy it."

The Signora wiped the coffee from her moustache and viciously tore another chunk off the loaf.

"So!" she observed again, "the sister has gone with her little Tedescho and left you penniless and in a foreign country without resources and friends; it is shameful. Was she not your sister I would have much to say. But very much."

"Please do not disturb yourself on my account," begged Mary. "I do not wish to return to England. I have no friends there and little acquaintance with my family . . . and I cannot be said to be without friends here . . ."

She smiled at the Signora who inclined her head majestically.

"I hope to retain my post with the theatre, playing the piano for rehearsals. I may also find pupils for the piano . . . and for singing . . ."

A rumbling and wheezing heralded Signor Matteo's entry into the conversation.

"Signorina," he announced, "in my opinion, which is not without weight, you and not your sister are the singer. I have heard . . ."

He was interrupted by his wife.

"In effect, I was right," she exclaimed, "that creature has abandoned you without a soldi . . ."

Mary shook her head.

"She believed she had provided for me, Signora. It is just that I find myself stupidly unable to make use of her provision. But I shall do very well . . . if I can find a very cheap room somewhere and there are a few pupils to be had."

Signora Matteo eliminated the crumbs which had lodged upon her bosom, rose to her feet and took Mary by the hand.

"Come!" she instructed and took her into the marble-floored hall. Above them the staircase curved gracefully into the upper regions, and the Signora set herself at the shallow steps with Mary racing behind her. They passed the appartmente signorile on the second floor where Mary's present lodging was, and went on up to the fourth floor of the house where, only slightly breathless, the Signora opened a door, and ushered Mary into a small chamber furnished with a high narrow bed, a huge carved chest of the kind in which one might expect to find a suffocated bride, and a table above which hung an ancient mirror. A small door gave on to a cupboard, and when the shutters surrendered to the Signora's rigorous handling, it could be seen that a balcony permitted the occupant of the room a view of the Calle, a glimpse of the canal to the right and the Campo San Luca to the left.

"It is yours . . ." announced the Signora, "and for a sum quite derisory, which you may pay when it is most convenient. I find few visitors who wish to climb this high. It is a favour to me if you will make use of it. A favour, I repeat . . ."

She scowled ferociously at Mary who shook her head and smiled in return.

"And as for those pupils whom you hope to obtain . . . would it not be of advantage to have . . . come with me!"

The Signora descended the stairs even faster than she had come up with Mary once more in tow. This time the objective was a small room on the first floor, which looked out on to a tiny, tank-like garden. It was cool and green with frescoed walls and a tiled floor. In one corner stood a pianoforte, surely the oldest that Mary had ever seen — Beethoven might have played upon one like it — but indubitably a pianoforte.

"Behold!" said the Signora, "in here you shall teach your pupils. And your first pupil will be my own god-child. Behold!"

"I did say," Mary said mildly, if a trifle breathlessly, "that my sister had not left me friendless . . . I spoke truer than I knew."

"It is nothing," said the Signora and her eyebrows dared Mary to contradict her. Mary did not try, but bent down and kissed her gratefully.

"You are so good to me you might be my mother."

"She is alive, your mother?"

"She died when I was born."

"Ah . . . poor child, poor child. She was Italian, no?"

"No."

Mary shook her head. The Signora looked puzzled.

"But you and your sister . . . you speak Italian like Italians; Italians of the Romagna."

"My father . . ."

"Also dead?"

"Since three years . . ."

"Ah, poor child, poor child . . ."

"He was a singer," explained Mary. "He lived in Italy for many years and my stepmother was Italian."

'Aha!"

The Signora pounced.

"She was the mother of that one, no?"

Mary shook her head again.

The Signora made another hideous grimace.

"Your full sister . . . the more shame to her! Your pardon . . . I should not say these things. I will send Francesca to move your baggage."

She swept across the hall like a tidal wave of mauve linen and crochet-lace, calling for Francesca. Mary sat down at the piano and played a few chords. The instrument was in tune and had a sweet, subdued tone. It seemed to cry out for Mozart. She sang 'Das Veilchen', and as she came to the end of the song she found Signor Matteo standing appreciatively in the door.

"A good voice," he wheezed, "strong and sweet, better than your sister's . . . such a pity . . ."

"Ah," Mary responded with a smile, "but you can't always be sitting down in an opera."

He shuffled away, shaking his head.

Rehearsals at the Benedetto began shortly after eleven. When Mary arrived that morning she found the theatre in a state of upheaval. Carpenters were hammering in the pit, painters removing the traces of the previous night's missiles, and on the stage a tearful member of the chorus, recently promoted to sing La Fiorella's role, was doing her best to make herself heard over the din. Mary's advent was welcomed and the company began to work with a will, rehearsing the soprano's scenes. Luncheon, for once, was forgotten. By three in the afternoon the stand-in was beginning to gain a little confidence, the company began to relax and Signor Carettoni was seen to smile for the first time that day. It was also to be the last. At ten minutes past three a file of soldiers marched in. The officer in charge did not wait for the end of the aria but bellowed in his thick Austrian-Italian,

"Carettoni!"

The manager who had found a seat in the gilt chairs near the orchestra jumped up and turned pale.

"What do you want of me?"

"This! Behold!"

The officer thrust a paper at him.

"The theatre is closed by order of the Governor," he announced, "and it will stay closed until further notice."

This doom pronounced he marched out, leaving the soldiers to eject the occupants by degrees. There ensued a scene of lamentations, tears, curses which echoed round the theatre with more passion than any engendered by the operas themselves. Mary dumped the costume in La Fiorella's dressing room, packed up the few possessions she had left behind and went to the office. Here, she hoped, she might be paid the money owed her. She found Signor Carettoni weeping into his hands. As she came in he lifted his head and glared.

"Her fault!" he exclaimed, "It is all the fault of that screeching little . . ."

He paused.

"If ever I see her again I'll tear out her throat," he went on, his hands curved into claws, "I will do the world this favour and hang happily . . . happily . . ."

He rose and shook his clenched fist under Mary's nose, standing on tip-toe to effect this.

"And if you would do me a favour . . . go . . . go now . . ."

"But," protested Mary, "I have never a soldi and you owe . . ."

"Ask it of your sister!" he screamed, "Go! Go!"

She left. There was really nothing else to do.

In the Campo di Benedetto Eduardo was waiting. He swept her into a chair in the café.

"Body of Bacchus, what a day, what a day!"

Belatedly Mary recalled the understage activities.

"Is everything safely bestowed?" she enquired.

"We have not slept," announced Eduardo conspiratorially, "we have not closed an eye. Before dawn we had the machine in a hundred thousand pieces ready for the handcart, and at midday it was ready for the first new printing. By the Blood, I have worked this day."

"Where? Or should I not ask?"

"Mother of God, but I should not tell . . . in the Calle di Ridotto under the Marionette Theatre."

"Are you to play there instead?"

His plump face assumed a clownishly exaggerated expression of regret.

"No, alas. The Marionettes have no music but a piper, and he is as thin as his pipe or there would be no space for him. In the theatre there is barely room for an audience let alone an orchestra."

Mary realised with a pang of guilt that she had been so concerned with her own impasse, that she had forgotten the effect that the closure must have on the rest of the company.

"What will you do?"

"Other arrangements can be made . . ."

He shrugged.

"All kinds visit the Marionettes . . . and it is dark inside."

"I meant what will you do yourself?"

He beamed at her.

"An angel of kindness to ask . . . I have some engagements. Enough to keep me alive. I have a brother who has a shop in the Mercerie. I can sell gloves for him if I am starving. And you? When do you leave for Vienna?"

"I am not going to Vienna."

"Then no doubt you return to La Inghilterra?"

Mary shook her head.

"No. I stay here."

Eduardo stared in consternation and pushed his plump fingers through his hair till he looked like Struwwelpeter.

"But . . . but what will you do?"

"Teach," said Mary firmly. "Either English or music."

She sounded more confident than she felt, but Eduardo, conversant with the difficulties of making a living in the moribund old city, was not deceived.

42

"You will starve," he prophesied, "without a doubt, starve you must and will . . ."

He stood up as if he could not contain his agitation and leaned on the metal table.

"Meess Porretusa," he began, "I cannot keep silent. I am a poor man with no money except what I earn with that . . ."

He nodded at the 'cello case which lay at his feet.

"I am fat . . ."

He patted the large expanse of waistcoat which gave colour to this assertion.

"I am no longer young, no longer handsome . . ."

His incorrigible honesty got the better of his instinct for drama.

"Though truth to tell," he interjected confidentially, "I was never more than passably good-looking . . ."

He raised his hand to silence Mary's protest (quite unnecessarily, as Mary found herself speechless).

"I have little or nothing to offer," he went on, "but a roof to cover you and a crust to share . . . but what I have is yours and myself, my unworthy and devoted self with it."

He bowed and sat down breathing rather fast and his brown eyes fixed anxiously upon her face.

"It isn't much, I know," he added, the grand manner abandoned, "but it would be better than nothing."

"Oh, Eduardo . . ." exclaimed Mary, thoroughly disconcerted, "I did not realise . . ."

She swallowed hard and set herself to the task of refusing his offer without wounding his amour-propre more than she could help. Eduardo made it easy by shaking his head at her and wagging his hand in a deprecatory gesture.

"I know . . . I know . . ." he said, "but remember, if you need me I would be proud, delighted . . . and now you must come and eat four grains of rice with me."

This economical proposition was the customary Venetian invitation to dinner. Mary refused gently; not only had she a good deal to attend to, but she felt that conversation could not help but be inhibited by what had just passed. Eduardo stood up to shake her hand when she rose to go.

"I am always to be found in the café on the Campo Morosini," he told her, "call on me if I can be of use to you in any way."

The last Mary saw of him was a rotund and rather melancholy figure standing hatless, watching her out of sight.

"What he really needs is a nice, plump little convent-bred girl, who will cook him all his favourite dishes and give him a baby every year," she told herself firmly to banish the overpowering compunction she felt. "He couldn't be doing with an English beanpole, whatever he may think now."

The British Consul was disengaged: a condition not unusual with him. Venice, lying passively resentful under the heel of Austria, was active neither socially nor commercially and her political activities were mostly illegal, and not such as to engage his official interest. In these circumstances there was little for the consul or his staff to do and, unless they had aesthetic leanings, less to entertain them. Mary found the consul on the verge of 'stepping round to the Piazza', but willing enough to postpone his coffee and gossip to hear her story. It was not every day a fair-haired goddess six feet tall appeared on his doorstep. He sent his man-servant for a glass of madeira wine and prepared to listen.

Mary's errand was simple; to register her presence in Venice with the consul in case her connection with the Benedetto might result in her vanishing suddenly into an Austrian prison. Such things were not unknown.

"You see, I have no relations in Venice . . . there is no one to wonder what has become of me."

"Quite, oh, quite . . ."

The consul sipped his wine and regarded her in a fatherly fashion.

"In the circumstances, Miss Porteous, do you not think it might be better to return to England?"

Mary shook her head.

"At present I have not the funds to do this."

44

"Dear me ... dear me! If it is not an impertinence may I enquire ... I mean, now the theatre is closed ... how can you..."

"I hope to obtain pupils for the pianoforte," said Mary more confidently than she felt. "My landlady has very kindly allowed me the use of her instrument..."

"Indeed! You must permit me to mention your name to my acquaintance. And may I suggest you insert an advertisement in the journal..."

At this point the door swung open to admit a young man with his hands full of papers, and the air of one who considers himself superior to his employment.

The sight of Mary brought him to an enquiring halt and the consul stepped britannically into the breach.

"Miss Porteous, may I present Mr Gerald Mawborough of our service. Miss Mary Porteous."

Mary held out her hand and Mawborough bowed over it.

"Porteous ... Porteous ... are you not the sister of La Fiorella of the Benedetto, Miss Porteous?"

"I am."

"I was fortunate enough to make your sister's acquaintance on one occasion ... in the company of Todaro del Doria."

The consul looked startled and a little annoyed.

"I understood you to say you had no relations in Venice, Miss Porteous."

"My sister is no longer in Venice."

"She has gone to Vienna, I believe," said Mawborough rather maliciously.

Mary raised her eyebrows.

"You are uncommonly well-informed, sir."

He smirked.

"La Fiorella's decision to leave was taken ... shall we say ... in public. It was my privilege last night to be there when she took it."

Mary suddenly began to laugh and the two men stared at her in surprise.

"Most unbecoming in me, I know ..." she admitted with some

45

difficulty, "but the opera is such a *pervasive* occupation. Tell me, did she plight her troth in recitative or in an aria? And how did the gallant captain reply? Was there a duet?"

She relapsed into helpless giggles again, a state in no way ameliorated by the bewildered gaze of the two men.

"I do beg your pardon," she managed at last, "I really do."

She rose and smiled down at them.

"I am obliged to you for your courtesy, sir, and depend on you to extract me from jail should the need arise."

"You can always sing to guide me to your cell," suggested the consul, anxious to meet his guest's mood.

"Naturally," she agreed, "and to the accompaniment of full orchestra and chorus."

She turned to Mawborough.

"I believe you said that Signor del Doria was a friend of yours?"

"I have that honour," assented Mawborough, "in fact I am engaged to dine in his company tonight."

"Ah," said Mary, "How convenient. I was about to ask you for his direction, but I am persuaded you will not object to giving him this when you see him tonight. My sister left it for him."

Mawborough bowed compliance and Mary handed him the pendent-case which she had packed carefully in a box and wrapped in paper.

"His letters returned, no doubt," speculated Mawborough and shook his head, "my poor, slighted friend."

"Let us hope for your sake, Mr Mawborough," said Mary sweetly, "that he does not express his chagrin in a ten minute aria in the key of E flat minor. Your dinner will get *so* cold."

A slight snort from the consul marked his appreciation of this flight, and Mary held out her hand to him.

"Good day to you, Mr Campion, and thank you."

When the servant had shown her out Campion laughed unkindly.

"Well, she certainly made you look no-how, Gerald. Very salutary!"

"Farouche creature!" said Mawborough contemptuously.

"But nice in her choice of errand-boys," the consul pointed out.

"And what a maypole of a creature," grumbled Mawborough, "nothing like her sister . . ."

"The more credit to her, then, if all I hear is true," said the consul. "Do you come to the Piazza?"

Mary crossed the Rialto and the action suddenly assumed a significance for her. The old life as her sister's shadow, chaperone, mentor and nurse was over. For the first time her situation became plain to her. She had no means worth the counting, her post with the opera company was gone, and the prospect of building up a sufficient clientele of pupils to save herself from starvation seemed remote. She would have to find some other source of income. Her mind ranged round the possibility of finding a post in a school. She could teach English, or music or drawing and had a smattering of German. Here too the outlook was gloomy; only the wealthy and well-born sent their daughters to school, and few of these found Venice under the occupation congenial. Their absence, indeed, was an important part of the Dimostrazione. She was wondering ruefully if the return of the pendent had been too costly a gesture, when her eye fell on a little shop at the corner of the Campo. The dingy window was crammed with watercolour sketches of the kind sold as souvenirs to summer visitors. Mary, always interested in pictures, stood for a moment to consider them. They were sorry daubs, feeble and washy, barely recognisable as views of the city.

"Lord," thought Mary, "I believe I could do better myself."

On the impulse she went into the shop, and the proprietor, whose reading of the journal had been discommoded by her presence at the window, was ready and smiling at her entrance. His smile faded at her offer to sell him similar (if better) paintings.

"I will make no promise," he shrugged, "how can I know? Bring me some to see."

He brightened when she laid out some of her dwindling store of lire on a supply of paint and paper.

47

"I will consider what you bring me," he agreed, "I can do no less, and . . ."

He gestured to a dark corner.

"I hire these to visitors for a few soldi."

He produced a small canvas stool and opened it up with a jerk, which sent a cloud of dust flying into the shaft of light from the window.

"You may borrow it . . . and for nothing."

Mary thanked him effusively and he smirked, brushing the cigar-ash from his worn velvet jacket.

"It is nothing . . . nothing . . ."

She had reached the door and, as was automatic with her in Venetian shops, had ducked her head to avoid braining herself on the lintel when he called after her.

"Signorina! Is it that you draw the figure? My customers like the figure in a picture."

Mary promised to remember this preference and hurried back to the Calle di Fuseri, where she ascended to her new quarters without meeting anyone, and unearthed her sketching equipment. No harm in making a start as soon as possible.

The place she planned to paint was at a junction of two canals, near the Calle di Ridotto. She had noticed the place on her wanderings round the city. The setting sun lit up some crumbling carvings on an old palazzo and there was a bridge which arched angularly over the opaque and gleaming water; beside the fondamente a gondola lay uncannily still. It was the kind of scene which visitors to Venice remembered. Quickly Mary blocked it in with her pencil and shaded it lightly; then she laid down a wash of green. She worked fast on the small piece of paper and in half an hour had a competent representation of the scene before her. All it required was 'the figure' and as she was considering, pencil in hand, the relative merits of a somnolent gondolier or a picturesque fruit-seller, neither of whom was actually present, he appeared. It was an urchin who came scurrying unexpectedly down the alleyway immediately opposite the bridge. He emerged panting into the evening sunlight, blinked and looked anxiously over his shoulder.

"And whose fruit-barrow has been honoured by the attentions of this poor little fellow?" asked Mary of no one in particular.

The ragged figure leaped up and across the bridge and paused in front of her.

"I have stolen nothing," he objected, and then grinned, "at least not this time. It is the filthy Whites who wish to see me . . ."

"The soldiers?" asked Mary, her pencil busy.

The urchin nodded and spat into the water.

"Pigs!" he declared, evidently reassured of her feelings by the tone of her voice. "Will the Signorina tell them she saw no one, I beg of her . . ."

He put out his hands in a universal beggar's gesture and then made to scamper away. Mary dropped her pencil, put out a long arm and gathered up a handful of ragged breeches.

"She can do better than that . . ."

She pushed the child down against the wall of the house and made him crouch there doubled up, half under the canvas stool.

"Sit there."

She spread her skirts over him and settled herself on the stool again.

"Just as well this did not happen in my grandmother's day," she commented, "her skirts would never have served."

As tall as she was, she avoided the extremes of fashion for fear of appearing, as she phrased it, like a fairground freak. Her skirts were full but her hoop was only a modest three feet or so. However, it served. The urchin vanished under a froth of french-blue muslin. Mary arranged the folds and placed her wooden paint box where it would prevent too close attention.

"Stay there . . . and keep silent," she muttered, "they're coming."

"I will even still my heart!" he promised in a muffled whisper.

"Don't move or come out until I tell you. Here they come. Company of cart horses!"

The Austrians came clattering down the narrow alleyway and emerged in front of the bridge, looking angrily and foolishly in all directions. There was a plump, red-faced Wachtmeister in charge of the squad and he shouted across the canal to Mary. He spoke in German. Mary looked at him blankly and returned to her work. He crossed the bridge and demanded in Italian of a kind whether she had seen a boy . . . a beggar-brat. Mary withdrew her attention from the picture and summoned up the arrogant and uncomprehending stare of her countrymen abroad.

"I'm English," she announced in that tongue, "I don't understand. Stand aside. I want to finish my painting."

She waved him aside imperiously and the Austrian, familiar with the attitude if not with the language, sheepishly obeyed her, taking a look at her drawing as he did so. His gaze sharpened at what he saw, he gave a hoarse shout of triumph and shouted across at his squad.

"There! There! He ran along to the left there! After him! This woman has put him in her picture!"

The squad clattered off in the direction he indicated into the dazzle of sunset. The sergeant took a last reassuring glance at the painting, and found that a swift and cruel thumbnail sketch of himself panting ungainly over the bridge had been added to it. His mouth, opened to thank her, shut angrily over his stained teeth and he was about to protest, when he again encountered that arrogant insular stare.

"Go away," said Mary, "you are in my light."

The Wachtmeister grunted and lumbered after his squad now labouring along the fondamente. Mary felt a faint stirring under the stool as if the urchin had heaved a sigh of relief. She watched the soldiers out of sight and carefully drew her monogram in the corner of paper. Then she levered out the pins which held it to the board. Still there was no sign that the soldiers were coming back. She was just about to tell the boy to come out when another figure appeared strolling along the fondamente from the east. He was a saturnine person, cloaked and unusually tall for an Italian. He turned on to the bridge.

"Stay where you are," Mary muttered under her breath and continued to remove the pins.

The newcomer strolled across the bridge, came to a halt at Mary's side and examined her work.

"A spirited piece of work, Signorina," he observed, "and tells us something as the cognoscenti declare all art should do."

He indicated the figure of the urchin in his striped shirt with a long forefinger.

"I wonder, does it tell me the truth. I have mislaid such an urchin."

Mary was about to subject him to the same treatment which had routed the Austrian, though this man's bright, sardonic eye suggested that he might not be so easy to vanquish, but her poise was a trifle ruffled by an undignified upheaval under her skirts as the urchin fought his way out.

"Signor! Signor!" he exclaimed, "We meet in a good hour!"

He scrabbled under his grimy striped shirt and produced a wad of manuscript which he handed to the newcomer with a bow. The man stowed it away and handed the bearer some silver.

"A thousand thanks, Signor.. .a thousand thanks."

"It seems to me," remarked his benefactor, "that they are owed more to the Signorina than to me."

The boy bowed with a flourish worthy of the Piazza and smiled blindingly at Mary.

"True, Signor, very true. I kiss your hand a thousand times! Signorina, I am your devoted servant to command!"

Mary stared down at her devoted servant in his bare feet, and his father's cut-down trousers precariously attached to his person by a string across the shoulder, and found her voice.

"It was nothing, Signorino," she returned and swept him a curtsey culled from the second act of *Cosi fan Tutte*, "a small service indeed to count you my friend."

"I am Angelo," announced her friend, "if La Gigantessa has need of my services she need only send . . . I will come."

He bowed again and pattered up the steps of the bridge; on the top he paused and looked back mischievously.

"Signorina La Gigantessa," he called, "would I had been ten years older!"

And with that pertinent observation he vanished into the alley from which he had appeared five minutes earlier.

"La Gigantessa, indeed!" said Mary indignantly.

"He will be one to reckon with in ten years," concluded the newcomer and laughed. "In all conscience, Signorina, you have made two good friends this evening. I, too, stand very much in your debt."

He tapped the breastpocket in which he had put the manuscript. Mary closed her paintbox and rose to empty the paintwater into the canal. The man examined her drawing again and chuckled.

"The Wachtmeister to the life," he said, "you are clever with your pencil."

Mary suddenly had a vision of the Tedescho discovering himself in the window of the shop near the Rialto and enquiring . . .

"If the picture amuses you, Signor, please accept it . . ."

"But I could not do that," he protested.

Mary folded the picture into tissue and held it out.

"It is of no value, Signor, except as a memento."

He smiled at her and she was suddenly, irrelevantly, aware that she had to look up at him.

"I would recall this occasion without a memento, Signorina, but it will give me great pleasure to take it."

He placed it carefully beside the manuscript and raised his widebrimmed hat.

"I hope we meet again," he said.

Mary was inclined to agree with him.

In the Calle di Fuseri Mary found Signora Matteo awaiting her return with a dish of canneloni and a glowering boy of about ten.

"My god-child, Orfeo," she announced," he wishes to learn music. Behold!"

It became clear to Mary before long that Orfeo's aunt had seriously misinterpreted his wishes. Despite his name he did *not* desire to learn music, and what was more, he intended to resist every effort made in this direction. Mary eyed him speculatively after the first few embattled minutes and declared a truce.

"Do you know a boy called Angelo?" she asked.

He glanced up at her, his attention caught.

"He's a gondolier's brother," said Orfeo, "he can fight."

"He is a friend of mine," Mary told him, "a good friend. Now, perhaps you will consider which of these notes is middle C?"

Orfeo considered.

3

". . . take this Jewel!"

Faust: GOUNOD

AT THE CAFÉ FLORIAN the party was nearly over. Groups of young men smoked cigars and discussed politics with a fire and passion in no way diminished by the fact that all of them were in profound agreement. Only the means to their common end were in dispute, but disagreement over these was enough to raise the temperature of the party, most of whom had drunk a bottle of wine apiece. In one group Gerald Mawborough listened rather blearily while a young man from Savoy sang the praises of Britannia as the Friend of Freedom, coupling Gerald's name with this sentiment.

"When the great day comes, my English friend, you will be with us on the barricades, defying tyranny!"

If Mawborough was sober enough to question the practicability of erecting barricades in a city of canals, he did not voice his doubts, but disengaged himself tactfully and went to join another group which had its heads together conspiratorially over a small round table, considering a broadsheet, rather unevenly printed and still smelling of printer's ink. At Mawborough's approach one of the group casually laid an ordinary newspaper over it. Del Doria looked up and greeted him politely but without enthusiasm.

"Trust I don't intrude," Mawborough began, "but I have an errand to you, del Doria. A packet from Miss Porteous."

He delved in his pocket but missed nothing of the glances which were exchanged at his mention of the name.

"Miss *Mary* Porteous..." he added as he produced the packet in its white paper, "she asked me to give you this."

Del Doria held it and frowned.

"You mean La Fiorella's sister, I collect. I can't recall that I ever met..."

"Very probably not," agreed Gerald, "she doesn't seem to go much about. Said it had been left by her sister or some such thing. Asked me to give it to you."

"I never realised there was a sister," remarked one of the men.

"Oh, yes," said another, "she was accompanist, companion, duenna..."

There was a ripple of laughter at that and Del Doria raised his eyebrows.

"No...no..." protested the speaker, "she was virtuous, the sister... virtuous as a nun. It was notorious."

He sighed comically and there was more laughter.

"And has La Fiorella not taken her 'duenna' to Vienna with her?" asked another of the men.

"No," said Gerald, "and she has been left damned inconveniently situated, what's more."

Del Doria looked up enquiringly.

"The theatre has been closed down," explained the Englishman, "and she has lost her post there. She hopes to find pupils for music and drawing but with Venice so thin of company..."

He shrugged.

"Doubtless she will have difficulties."

"And doubtless La Fiorella's sister will find a way to overcome them?" came from the man on del Doria's right.

"As to that," said Gerald waspishly, "I doubt if she will find it easy. She is certainly no beauty, a great yellow-haired maypole of a creature..."

De Doria frowned suddenly at that description and put the packet unopened into his pocket.

"I'm obliged to you, Signor Mawborough," he said, "most kind..."

The dismissal was unmistakable and Gerald's face reddened as he bowed and retired; but his malice focused on Mary for being the cause of his receiving such a snub, not on the author of it.

He resolved to see her in the canal before he would run another errand for her.

Later that night del Doria opened the packet in his lodging. He found the blue leather case and a note in Mary's neat, square hand.

My sister left this with me to be returned to you. In the circumstances it was not possible to retain such a gift.

MP

Del Doria sneered : pretty talking — La Fiorella had managed to reconcile a ruby and diamond brooch and a pair of pearl earrings with her tender conscience — unless they too were in the case. He opened it and found nothing but the pendent, though a shake produced a slight rattle which suggested that there might be some object under the velvet tray. He lifted it and a heavy gold and emerald signet ring rolled into his hand. He stared at it in bewilderment; he had never seen it before in his life. He looked in the case again but there was nothing there except a paper jammed into the bottom. He opened and recognised the sprawling hand of La Fiorella. He could read English :

Dear Mary, [La Fiorella had written] I've decided to go to Vienna tonight with Steiger : I think he might marry me if I play my cards properly. [Del Doria's bewilderment gave way to amusement] and I am so bored with the Theatre and Venice and the Opera and all the travelling. I have taken the money because I earned it and I need it but you can sell this pendent for enough to get home and a bit over. I asked the Jeweller in the Mercerie. I have left you Grandfather's ring too. It is too big for me. I'll write when I get to Vienna and you can come and stay may be some day.
     In great haste,
        yr affekT. sister,
          Flora.

Del Doria stared at the signet ring in dismay and read the

bald, ungracious little note again. Then he considered the note which had come with the packet, and compared the signature with that on a water-colour sketch which was propped against the mirror above his chimney piece. After a moment's thought he put the ring in a drawer in his dressing chest, called for two working candles and sat down to write a letter.

It was nearly three weeks later that Mary opened the front door of the Calle di Fuseri house as softly as she could. In one hand she carried a folder of unsold paintings, in the other a paper containing chicken-blood sausage still warm from the cook-shop. It was her first food for some thirty-six hours and her mouth watered at the thought of it. She shut the door as quietly as she could. It was not because her rent was unpaid; that was the first call upon her resources. It was to avoid a hospitality from the Matteos which to her sharpened sensibilities verged on charity. If she had foolishly chosen to starve for a scruple, Mary considered, she should not accept too much help. The situation was after all of her own making. Food of a sort could be had for a few soldi when she sold a painting. When spring came and the first of the visitors, it would be easier. The worst just now was the cold : but the Signora had supplied plenty of counterpanes. The huge latch slipped into place under cover of a seller of hot chestnuts, who was advertising his wares in a manner which suggested that he was being torn apart by fiends with red hot pincers. Mary tiptoed across the hall to the staircase to which she owed her present dinner. A painting of it bearing 'the figure' dressed as for a masquerade had persuaded the shopkeeper to add just one more souvenir to his stock. The proceeds would buy food for the next day too and on Friday Orfeo would . . . might come.

She had almost reached the first steps when the Matteos' door swung open and the vast accusing figure of the Signora stood there portentous in purple satin and a six-foot hoop.

"Signorina!" she called, "Signorina! For days you have not vouchsafed us one word. In what way have we offended?"

Mary turned and dropped her parcel in embarrassment.

57

"Signora, how can you suggest such a thing?"

But the Signora's eyes were on the tiled floor where the oily paper had opened to reveal its contents.

"Maria of the Skies! That you should buy such stuff! You will die writhing in the belly-ache. Come!"

She swooped on Mary and drew her into the warm kitchen . . . at that time of the year it was the only warm room in the whole palazzo.

"Behold! Sit down and eat. My friend to be eating from cookshops . . . ugh!"

A plate of steaming golden polenta appeared before her and delicious crisp fried sprats were sprinkled over it: a ladleful of sauce followed, sharp with tomatoes and peppers, aromatic with oregano and garlic . . .

"Eat!" ordered the Signora with mock sternness and Mary was only too glad to obey.

"Eat, before your bones come through your skin . . ." said the Signora accusingly, and pulled at the slack now available in Mary's green serge bodice. One cannot live on chicken-blood sausage for three weeks and not lose flesh.

A saucer with sticky mandorlato and a glass of warm red wine both appeared as if by magic.

"Pappa! I have caught her! She is here."

Signora Matteo rarely shouted. She did not need to; from her person emerged a voice which carried like a bronze bell. In their day Signor and Signora Matteo had been the principal bass and contralto at the Teatro Fenice.

"Do not forget the letter!" he rumbled from the inner room. The cold of the Venetian winter drove him to take to his bed for much of the day.

"I have not forgotten," called his wife. "Behold! It is here."

Mary was thinking as she always did how their conversation resembled recitative, when a large square envelope was placed with a flourish against her wine glass.

"Since this morning I watch for you."

Mary slipped her thumb under the seal which was of purple wax and splashed generously over the paper. The device was of some crouching heraldic beast which she did not recognise. The contents were a single sheet of scented paper covered with an elaborate handwriting. Signora Bianca Murano presented her compliments to Signorina Porteous, and begged to inform her that the Signorina had been highly commended as an instructor in music and drawing. Signora Murano found herself in need of such an instructor for the education of her daughter Giannina and her younger son Pietro. If Signorina Porteous was prepared to consider such a position perhaps she would have the goodness to call at the Palazzo Murano during the morning of Thursday.

Wordlessly Mary showed the letter to the Signora, who had been indicating massive incuriosity on the other side of the table. She took it in her hand, withdrew a pair of pince-nez from the purple satin folds on her bosom and gave the letter her fullest attention. At the end she gave vent to a complicated noise at once gratified and regretful.

"We will lose you!" she exclaimed and extended her range effortlessly to inform the Signora, "It is good news, Pappa, but we will lose her! Alas! Alas!"

"But Signora I have not ... perhaps they will not ..."

Signora Matteo continued to communicate with her husband. "It is a post as institutrice with the Muranos ..."

Pappa made subterranean noises indicating approval.

"An old family ... Venetians of the republic," explained his wife, "and rich yet. Huge estates near Padua and in the Veneto. You are fortunate Signorina, fortunate indeed. And who is this friend who has done you such a good turn?"

"If it is not you ..." said Mary and the Signora shook her head in denial, "... then I cannot imagine. It has me in a puzzle. Apart from you and Pappa who are a host in yourselves, I have no friends in Venice."

"No doubt you will discover tomorrow ... and today ... this instant ..."

A little heap of coins appeared before Mary's plate.

"... you will immediately redeem your dark blue silk gown, your blue muslin, your blue velvet walking dress, the brocade dress with the scarlet silk fringe and your grey woollen cloak.

59

All these you will need! Behold . . . do not refuse me for you will repay from the princely salary which doubtless you must receive. No . . . no! I will not hear of refusal."

"But Signora . . ."

"No buts . . ."

"Signora they are not in the Monte di Pieta. I have sold them."

The Signora nodded.

"I am aware. Not to the pawn shop but to the clothes shop in the Calle della Fava. She has not sold them. They are by far too generously made for our Venetian midgets!"

The Signora was built on lines which if they did not match Mary's for height quite surpassed them for depth and breadth; a trace of contempt could be heard in the reference to midgets.

"It is enough," she declared, "you will buy them back and leave off that green which becomes you not and depresses me to the cutting of throats. One must present a respectable appearance to such people . . ."

In Venice shops could be said to be shut only when the proprietors were asleep, so that Mary's wardrobe was fully restored before she went to bed. In the morning the heavy sky promised rain, so she put the grey cloak over the blue velvet dress and left her only hat in the chest. The Palazzo Murano lay on the other side of the Grand Canal on the west side of the Rio delle Muneghette. It would have been simpler to take a gondola but Mary had no soldi to spare; she would walk. She set off for the Rialto. On the Riva del Vin on the other side a barrel organ was playing waltzes, and a boy in a red cap and wooden shoes who had been selling cakes to the soldiers on the quay, grabbed another urchin and waltzed, wooden shoes and all, up and down the Riva, under the amused gaze of the soldiery. The pair in their wild career nearly cannoned into Mary. The red-capped one looked up in dismay.

"Scusate, bella giovane . . ."

He broke off, beamed in delight and swept off the cap.

"It is La Gigantessa : well met, Signorina ! How may I serve you?"

"Angelo!"

"Himself."

Mary put out her hand and Angelo kissed it with aplomb. Then he fell in beside her abandoning his dancing partner without a backward glance.

"You go whither?" he enquired.

"To the Palazzo Murano."

"On foot, Signorina?" he exclaimed, "you will be wet to the bone. Behold, it has begun to rain."

This had not escaped Mary's notice.

"Permit me to obtain you a gondola."

Before she could prevent him he clattered to the quayside and called out shrilly,

"Barca ! Barca ! Alessandro !"

By the time Mary reached the quayside herself Alessandro had manoeuvred his craft alongside and was waiting, his hat at a jaunty angle and ragged mittens covering the chilblains, which seemed to be a universal complaint during a Venetian winter.

"My brother!" said Angelo proudly, "he will take you as fast as a dolphin."

Mary produced her purse from the reticule on her arm.

"My friends, I have no more than a few soldi and that will be no return for your trouble. I regret..."

Alessandro waved his hand in a grand gesture.

"You have helped my brother, Signorina...now let us aid you. It is cruelly wet. This poor boat is yours!"

And indeed it had come on to rain heavily. Angelo held the boat to the quay wall and Alessandro handed her in with a smile which was the very echo of his brother's.

"This will be a pleasure, Signorina..."

He put her carefully on the leather-covered bench under the hood.

"We have heard much of La Gigantessa," he told her, "her heavenly kindness, her hatred of Austrians, her undoubted artistic talents and her quickness of thought. A delight to meet with you."

He smiled and retreated to his post on the stern and the vessel glided out into the broad canal among the traffic of the morning. milk-boats and wood-boats, luxurious private gondolas, a chugging vaporetto, a heavy river-boat from Mestre laden with cabbages and crewed apparently by a dog . . . it seemed no time until the gondola scraped alongside the green-stained steps which led up to the heavy bronze-panelled doors of the Palazzo Murano. Angelo leaned out and held the side and Alessandro helped her ashore. She thanked them as gracefully as gratefully, picked up her blue velvet skirts and made her way up to the doors. Above her she saw a foreshortened view of grotesque carvings and elegant balconies, as if the palazzo glanced down casually at this latest visitor in a procession which had begun three hundred years earlier. At the foot of the steps the brothers waited to see her admitted, smiling in their uncannily identical fashion.

The doors swung inward revealing a bent and untidy ancient of days girdled in a grimy baize apron, who bowed her in with Venetian ceremony. Later she was to bless Angelo for his impulse, for to arrive in this way at the grand entrance of the house established her in a curious fashion as a person of standing, which a less spectacular entrance through the door off the Campo San Pantalon could never have done.

The hall was uncompromisingly beautiful and unlike most Venetian houses it gleamed with fresh paint. It ran the length of the building and was lit by seven, high, narrow windows which gave on to the Rio delle Munneghette. The light reflected from the waters outside, played constantly and fascinatingly among the plaster-work, which elaborated the proportions of the ceiling. The floor was chequered in green and white stone, oiled and polished until it shone like water. From the centre of the wall opposite the windows a graceful double staircase rose to a gallery, which ran round the four sides of the hall above the level of the windows. The three blank walls up there were used as a gallery for paintings and sculptures, and from the other side three superb pedimented doorways gave on to the various suites of rooms in the older part of the palazzo, where the grace of the eighteenth century gave way to the quirks and secrecies of earlier periods. From the hall below arched entrances veiled in brocade led to the ball-room, the banqueting hall and other superb and mostly unfrequented suites of reception rooms. An obscure door to the right of these hinted at the existence of the kitchens.

However, Mary did not learn the geography of the house at the first glance; in fact in that first glance she saw nothing but the motley collection of people milling about in the hall : Bianca the flower-woman with a basketful of the huge plate-like posies favoured by the Venetians, sat on the bottom step of the staircase hoarsely claiming her right to interview her namesake, the mistress of the house. A thin woman with a red tip on her nose stood aloofly in the centre of the hall clutching a velvet-bound book in one hand and a swatch of silks and brocades in the other. A priest conversed solemnly with a needle-nosed little man who had lawyer written all over him. A cluster of basket-laden women displayed vegetables and chickens and loaves to one another, talking volubly and all at the one time of their respective and superlative merits. Mary knew the cadaverous individual with the tattered volume of astrology under his arm. Signor Carettoni had been one of his customers though, perhaps understandably, the soothsayer had foreborn to inform him of the impending disaster at the Teatro Benedetto. Maids in caps and aprons, and untidy manservants trotted to and fro across the hall and up and down the stairs with items of furniture, luggage and armfuls of clothes, chattering and arguing over where they were to be bestowed. The elderly butler looked at the scene and sighed.

"The Signora is occupied this morning . . ."

Mary looked at the scene in dismay.

"Is she to see all the people here?"

The butler peered at her uncertainly.

"Who can say? The housekeeper who should deal with these people would not come to Venice because her third cousin is married to an Austrian and people make unkind remarks, you understand. I am old and nearly blind and no one heeds what I say. My lady is easily overset... I will tell her that you are here. Follow if it please you."

He sighed and hobbled off with Signora Murano's letter in his hand. Mary followed him up the first flight of stairs and found herself in a beautiful, almost empty room in which there was only a charcoal brazier, a faded Persian rug and a day-bed upholstered in atrocious green and yellow stripes, upon which reclined Signora Murano. Mary's immediate impression was one of softness; soft black hair, soft skin, enormous soft brown eyes. Even her clothes were of gentle pastel-coloured materials. Before the daybed stood a young man over whose outstretched arms were draped lengths of silk in blues and lilacs. Over the carved back of the daybed bent the owner of the silk, extolling its virtues in terms positively poetic. Signora Murano looked up distractedly as the butler came in.

"Ah, Guiseppe, it's you... I cannot decide between the french blue and the violet... it is so difficult. What do you think?"

"Signorina Porretuse, Signora..." said Guiseppe.

Mary advanced to the daybed and the Signora reached up a tiny plump hand glittering with rings.

"So happy to greet you, dear girl... I hope you will be happy with us... Giannina and Pietro cannot contain themselves with... Tell me, my dear, which would you choose... I mean to have a walking-dress for summer."

Mary looked down at the billowing figure on the daybed and wondered what possible use the Signora might have for a walking-dress.

"The blue," she said without hesitation, "the violet is too harsh for you... but better than either a yellow... a deep yellow."

The Signora sat up at this daring suggestion.

"Yellow? But I never wear yellow. It will make me look a hag."

Mary shook her head.

"No such thing, Signora, with your hair and your eyes and your clear olive skin ... it will be most becoming to you."

The silk merchant gave Mary a look of acute dislike.

"Alas, Signora, I have no yellow with me."

"Then bring some tomorrow ... muslins too. You know, my dear, you could be quite right ... a good, clear yellow ..."

Signora Murano waved dismissal at the silk merchant and indicated that Mary should sit beside her. Mary glanced at the retreating figures and Guiseppe hovering unhappily in the doorway.

"Does the Signora intend to see all those people in the hall?" she asked.

"What people? I don't want to see any people."

"There are a number waiting."

"Who are they?"

Tremulously Guiseppe began to tick them off on his fingers.

"... and the parroco and the advocate to see the Paron," he finished.

His mistress looked horrified.

"But I cannot possibly see all those ... it is too much. I should be prostrated ... Guiseppe how could you permit such a thing?"

An argument ensued in which Guiseppe tearfuly pleaded age, overwork and incapacity, and the Signora lamented a cruel fate, which burdened her with delicate health and beloved ancient incompetents and instructed him to send them all away upon the instant ...

"... and who was it admitted them?" she demanded. "Who permitted such a thing to happen?"

"They came in by the side door ... I knew nothing of it. Of a sudden they were there. I have tried to send them away but they will not hear me ..." he quavered.

Mary intervened.

"Have I your permission, Signora, to send them off?"

"My dear girl ... how kind, how considerate ... how ..."

Mary did not wait on further adjectives. A brief consultation with Guiseppe and she re-entered the hall, where the commotion was such, that it had attracted the displeased attention of a grey-haired man in his fifties who looked down sourly from the balcony.

"My good friends," she announced in carrying tones, "the Parona regrets that she can see no one today. She wishes me to assure you of her continuing favour, and begs that you will take a glass of wine and a biscuit in the kitchen before you leave."

After an astonished moment the crowd converged on Mary offering such inducements to channelling that 'continued favour', that gave her a very poor idea of the absent House-keeper. Mary resolutely declined posies, sweets, loaves, scent, ribbons, eggs, hens, an aubergine of mammoth proportions and a free horoscope and slowly succeeded in shepherding them through the kitchen door. She returned to the hall smiling con-spiratorially at Guiseppe, who thanked her very heartily and bade her welcome, thrice welcome to the household. "For I am but a poor old man . . . I cannot deal with people in the towns."

"I would like to be associated with that," put in the grey-haired gentleman from his vantage point on the gallery,

"The Paron . . ." whispered Guiseppe.

". . . and if you reduce my children to order with the same ease and tact, you are most heartily welcome even if you never teach them a note of music. Guiseppe, I have my desk but no chair, my books have been arranged by an illiterate so that I must stand on my head to find what I need; there is no writing paper and I require my chocolate. This house is like a madhouse."

"Behold me, Signor. All comes in the twinkling of an eye!"

Guiseppe went through the service door in the wake of the crowd, while Mary made her way up the staircase to greet her new employer.

"You are Signorina Porretuse of course," he informed her, and kissed her hand, "you are indeed uncommonly tall. Have you seen my wife?"

Mary nodded, wondering briefly who it was had mentioned her height.

"In that case I too bid you welcome in whatever capacity you care to act, tutor, major-domo, musician . . ."

"Signor," Mary interrupted him, "your wife has not said to me that ... there has been no decision about ..."

"You have not the slightest need to tell me that," said Murano rather acidly and began to beat a retreat to his quarters. "You have evidently decided that you can be of use to us and I confidently expect to meet you at dinner. You will find, Signorina, that this household has an infinite capacity to absorb decisions. From pressure of business I have ceased to take them on domestic matters where my knowledge is limited; my wife lacks the ability to take them, and my children are children still and thus take ill-considered ones. And Guiseppe, my very old and dear friend should long ago have returned to his village and can no longer see when one needs to be made. Till I see you again ..."

The huge door closed on him and the hovering figures of the advocate and the priest. Guiseppe appeared with a tray on which steamed a pot of chocolate and began to labour up the staircase.

"Friend," said Mary from the half-landing, "as you have said yourself, you are no longer young. From my observation this house swarms with able-bodied servants. Can no one be found to carry that for you?"

The old man stopped and looked at her rather apprehensively.

"Perhaps Marco?" he suggested.

"Understood."

Mary went through the service door beyond the staircase and entered the kitchen, which at that point resembled nothing so much as a café in full clatter and cry.

"Marco!"

The buzz died and a sheepish figure disentangled himself from a passionate encounter with a fruitseller. Mary considered him. He wriggled unhappily.

"You have a jacket?" she enquired and as if she had rubbed a lamp a green livery jacket emerged from the mêlée. Marco fumbled at his shirt-buttons and scrambled into the garment.

"Take up the Paron's chocolate," said Mary and turned her gaze upon the rest of the company. The guests began to recall urgent appointments elsewhere in the city and to slip through the back door. The household staff sprang into energetic (if not very productive) action under that cool, amused, blue eye. Mary identified a cook — he was a Neapolitan — and three subdued and adoring cookmaids, a giggle of black-aproned housemaids and two other young Venetians wearing, or rather, not wearing, a livery like that of Marco. She nodded, smiled enigmatically and withdrew upon Marco's heels leaving the kitchen a-bubble with bewilderment, indignation and speculation : however, the work of the household began to go forward.

The interview with Signora Murano which followed this interlude was a trifle disjointed. This was possibly because the parties to it were at cross-purposes. Mary was at some pains to discover whether in fact she had been engaged, while the Signora, taking this unimportant matter for granted, was concerned to impress her new dependent with the delicacy of her constitution, which rendered it impossible for her to play the role she would have wished in the care of her children and the management of her household. When Mary enquired anxiously if the Signora considered her qualifications sufficient, that lady gestured her to a seat on the day-bed and launched into a minute by minute account of her last confinement. When Mary produced her recommendations, the Signora waved them aside and began a long diatribe on the iniquities of Venetian servants. At length Mary was encouraged to suppose, on being the recipient of an account of Signor Murano's latest infidelity, that her presence in the household was now an accepted thing.

"... for my dear, now you are come perhaps I may have a little time for my music; I shall expect you to help me as well as the children of course ..."

Mary ventured to insert in the account of the Signora's youthful triumphs at the drawing-room instrument, an enquiry as to what her duties were to be. Signora Murano billowed to her feet and declared that despite the exertion, she must give herself the pleasure of presenting her beloved children to their new preceptor. They then set off across the vast expanses of mosaic floor at a pace suitable for a delicate constitution and a vast hoop.

"I have seven children," the Signora explained, as Mary opened both leaves of the double door to permit the passage of the hoop. "My oldest son Antonio is in Rome, Giannina and Pietro will be in your care. Giannina is seventeen and Pietro sixteen. Bianca, Alberto, Teresa and Mario are still in the country. We have a house near Padua and the air is better there . . ."

They passed the door of Signor Murano's retreat just as it opened to permit the departure of the parroco. He greeted the Signora ecstatically, and demanded to be acquainted with every detail of her life since she had last been in Venice, and also to know the state of health of the whole family. As she seemed more than happy to oblige him in every particular, Mary prepared to wait. Her new employer (or so she hoped) emerged and stood smiling at the group. He edged up beside Mary and mentioned in a voice so quiet that it was almost like a thought in her head.

"You are not a Catholic, Signorina?"

"No," she replied, a little startled.

"The children are in the schoolroom. Through that door and at the end of the corridor. I think you ought to go before the parroco begins to put you to the question."

She glanced at him quickly and saw that his thin pleasant face wore a slightly amused expression. He then joined in the conversation and drew the attention of both his wife and the priest in his direction. Mary slipped through the door and found she had moved back in time, into the sixteenth century. The walls were panelled, the doors low and the floor worn and uneven. She closed the door and moved quietly along to the end of the passage. Obscure Murano ancestors considered her from their vantage points on the panels. The end door was slightly open. Mary pushed it, and discovered one of her prospective charges being rather clumsily embraced by a soberly dressed individual, not much older than she was. Mary was taken aback and uncertain whether to beat a retreat or take a stand upon propriety but, before she could come to any conclusion about her duties here, the embrace was terminated abruptly as the young man realised he was being observed.

Mary's experience of amorous occasions was limited and such as it was, was coloured by the opera. She looked with interest at the pair, somehow expecting the young man to break into torrents of defiance and deathless devotion : instead he flushed scarlet and gulped.

"I take it you are *not* Signorina Pietro?" Mary observed, "Is he at hand? I should like to meet him."

The bashful one muttered incoherently and blundered through a door in the far corner. Giannina, instead of imploring Mary with clasped hands and an impassioned vibrato not to betray her guilty secret to her harsh parents, giggled and came forward with admirable aplomb to greet her new governess.

"You must be our new Meess," she concluded. "What an introduction! Whatever must you think!"

Mary considered the dark, lively face laughing up at her.

"I think you should throw him back and let him grow," she said in English.

"Please?" enquired Giannina, her head on one side, "I know no English . . . Pietro knows a little. He says it is the language of freedom but it is very difficult to learn . . ."

"What I said is of no importance. The young man who did not wait for an introduction?"

"He's my brother's tutor, Signor Lorenzo," confided Giannina drawing Mary over to a settee, "he is supposed to teach Pietro German and French, but Pietro is so Italianissimo that he refuses to learn a word of either . . ."

She giggled again.

"Il poverino, Lorenzo . . . he gets so discouraged."

"Such was not my impression," said Mary drily just as the other door swung open and Pietro came in. He was tall, nearly as tall as she was herself, and as dark as his sister but without her vivacity. On his face was an expression which, so he hoped, displayed his weariness with an unsatisfactory world, but which to Mary, as yet unacquainted with his storm-tossed soul, looked uncommonly like the sulks. She held out her hand and smiled.

"You must be Pietro," she told him, at which venture into the obvious he sneered, but felt obliged by convention to give her hand a perfunctory shake in the English manner.

"I *won't* say I hope we will all be great friends," said Mary. "That is to ensure that we set to the throat-cutting. But I hope we can work together comfortably."

Pietro struck an attitude and stared out of the window.

"All I hope," he remarked sombrely, "is that some day Venice will be free from Austrian tyranny."

Giannina giggled.

Mary confronted by a political manifesto smiled brightly.

"Well, let's make a start by tidying up this room," she said briskly and gubernatorially indicating the chaos of half-unpacked cases and trunks, and the muddle of clothes, books and tennis rackets which strewed the furniture, "when that is done we can make plans to outwit the Tedeschi . . ."

If she was to be a governess, a governess she would be.

4

"Take this ring I give you . . ."

La Somnambula: BELLINI

IN A VERY FEW days after Mary's arrival she found that the Murano household had thankfully cast their burdens upon her shoulders. Signor Murano was no gentleman of leisure, and he spent much time in his study attending to a huge correspondence or closeted with a curious assortment of visitors. He also made frequent train journeys, so that taking one thing with another, his family saw very little of him. Mary quickly found an affection for his wife, but this partiality did not blind her to the fact that Signora Murano was the most idle woman she had ever met and was prepared to cherish anyone who would, like Mary, take over her duties and leave her to enjoy a comfortable, gossipping inactivity, As for the rest of the household, they responded to a hand laid on the rein and came to Mary more and more for the decisions which were required from day to day, and which no one else, as the Paron had predicted, seemed ready to make. Guiseppe abdicated gratefully an authority he had been unable to exert. Engaged (she hoped) as a governess-chaperone, Mary found herself willy-nilly becoming a kind of major domo.

Revisiting the Calle di Fuseri she mentioned this dilemma. Signora Matteo nodded comfortably.

"It is what one would expect," she observed, "the English, they are so strong-minded. How should things be otherwise?"

"But . . ." Mary protested, "they know nothing of me. And they trust me with everything. It is being foolish beyond permission. I could rob them of their eyeteeth!"

The Signora dismissed this assertion with contempt and

reverted to another of Mary's problems, in which she had taken a burning and romantic interest.

"And how are you to act in the matter of il poverino, Lorenzo?"

As a matter of fact Mary had acted already. She had not informed her employers of the situation, considering that they might well take a very serious view of what she considered to be a trivial incident, and this could blight the career of il poverino. She also considered that her new charge, whom privately she had judged a minx, was much more at fault in the matter than the young man. Indeed, Giannina had said as much. Consequently, after considering the matter for a week (during which time that young man had expected to be hurled forth with contumely at any moment), Mary had taken him aside and suggested that he might find more congenial employment elsewhere. This possibility was underlined by a glowing testimonial, lavish in its praise if somewhat vague in its specifications, written by Mary and signed by Signor Murano, who read accurately between the lines and hid his amusement behind a bland agreement with Mary, that Pietro might respond better to an older man. In the meantime he might devote his time to studying English with Mary.

Mary supervised the rejected suitor's departure to his home and Giannina saw him go without regret; on the whole she found her new governess more entertaining and less demanding. Lorenzo in the train to Mestre renounced all women and decided to enter the Church.

One day during the following week the Paron was at home and uncharacteristically at leisure. It occurred to him to discover how it was with his family. It was, moreover, the end of the month and he intended to cast up his accounts. He paid a visit to his wife's sitting room where he drank a cup of chocolate, discussed the adultery of her best friend with the husband of another and enquired after her health. Having listened in an inattentive silence to the reply he rose and requested the household account books.

"The accounts?" said Signora Murano. "Oh, I have given them to my dear Meess weeks ago. She will let you have them."

Her husband raised his eyebrows.

"She helped me at first," explained his wife, "but I made so many errors that it was easier that she should keep the tiresome things till Tia Caterina can take them again. And she prepares the menus so she must have the money for the market, and she pays the servants because it gives me a headache when they come all crowding into my room . . ."

The Paron went in search of the governess. He found her in the schoolroom together with Giannina, who was practising her scales and exercises, while Mary accompanied her upon the piano. Pietro apparently oblivious to this was translating a passage from Galliciolli into laboured English. Signor Murano raised his eyebrows at this scene of industry and mentioned his errand. Mary rose and took the account books from her desk.

"If I may trespass in your domain for a minute or two?"

He sat down in the chair by the desk and began to leaf through the books, nodding at Mary and his daughter.

"Please to continue."

The practice was resumed but not for very long. A tap at the door heralded Guiseppe who had come for the daily conference over meals and household matters. With a nod of permission from the Paron they discussed the pressing necessity to oil the terrazzo floor in the hall, the sewing of rings upon the new brocade curtains to replace those in the bookroom, the problems involved in cleaning the huge windows which overlooked the Rio del Muneghette and other trivialities which had not before been brought to the attention of the master of the house. The duties of the staff for the day were laid down and the menus for the following day discussed and approved . . .

Mary was conscious of the neat presence at her desk running a thin dry finger down her columns of figures, and recalled a problem which she could not solve.

"Signor," she interrupted him, "Guiseppe tells me it is necessary to send for wine from Padua, from Monte Colon. If you would be so good . . ."

"I will attend to it."

The Paron's head did not move from the contemplation of the acounts. The conference went on to cover the purchase of linen for sheets to be sewn by the maids, as soon as they had finished the hemming of holland for furniture covers. It was the Paron's turn to interrupt.

"Holland? Furniture covers?" he enquired, his finger on an item in the book. "What are these?"

"For when you return to Padua," she explained, "Signora Murano was distressed to find that the silk covers in her sitting room were much faded . . . and the velvet in the small salon . . ."

He nodded. He also noted that Giannina, evidently accustomed to these morning interruptions had picked up some needlework and was stitching with an air of conscious virtue, which made her father's mouth twitch with amusement.

Mary dealt quickly with the rest of the morning's problems; the candlesmoke stains on the ceiling of the dining saloon, the unwound clock in the music room and the regrettable matter of young Antonio . . . on this Mary allowed no argument.

"No wine with his dinner for a week," she decreed, "and he must lose his free day."

Guiseppe bowed and departed.

"And what has young Antonio done?" enquired that sinner's employer.

"He was given permission to attend his sister's wedding," explained Mary, "and he returned in an inebriated condition . . ."

The paron shrugged.

"A wedding is an occasion for wine and rejoicing, Meess Maria . . . you are severe!"

"He went in his new livery," Mary enlarged, "having no other clothes suitable. Unfortunately he saw fit to try to sober himself by bathing in the Canalazzo. He now requires another new livery, his old one being fit for nobody but a freak in a side-show."

Her listeners laughed.

"And . . ." she added vigorously, "this time *I* will choose the cloth."

Before he left, the Paron found another item which puzzled him.

"This I do not understand," he told her, and pointed at a recurrent item, "Marco: basket-money."

"Marco goes to the market in the early morning," she explained. "I told him if he accounted properly for the money I gave him he could have a percentage of what was spent. And he does."

"And this prevents him taking the customary commission?" The Paron's eyebrows were high with disbelief.

"As to that . . ." said Mary honestly, "I couldn't say. But he knows that I check the prices at the market most days . . . and the bills have gone down . . ."

The Paron agreed to this with an enthusiasm which sat oddly upon him. Before he left the room there were two further calls upon Mary: the first was to interview a number of applicants for the post of laundry-maid (vacated by the former incumbent owing to a pressing engagement with the midwife), and the second came from the maid who attended upon the Parona with a request that Mary should visit a confectioner in the Calle dei Fabbri and purchase a species of sugared almonds which the Signora found especially toothsome. In the interim Mary found time to correct Pietro's exercise, hear him read a passage from the *Adventures of Nigel* and set Giannina to practise her piece upon the harp.

The Paron slipped the books back into her desk and left. When a few minutes later she went to enter the day's transactions which arrived by the hand of Marco, she found a neat tick on each column and a slip of paper which instructed her to increase her own emolument by half as much again. This so startled her that she did not notice that Marco had a note for Pietro; it must have contained an assignation, for within a few minutes he had made his excuses and begged permission to take the air before the gong rang for luncheon.

Later that day the Paron sent for Mary to come to his study. "I have been very much at fault," he told her bluntly. "I had not realised that the whole care of the household had been cast upon your shoulders. This is quite ineligible ..."

He glanced up at her with a sardonic smile.

"Not..." he added, "that this burden appears to have discomposed you in any way. However, it is time you had some relief. I have just written a letter to our housekeeper, Tia Caterina, singing your praises in a fashion which will bring her here hotfoot, despite her third cousin's lamentable taste in husbands..."

Mary laughed at this novel method of coercing his dependents and her employer raised his eyebrows in a manner she was coming to understand.

"Signorina! Signorina!" he warned, "Tia Caterina is no laughing matter! However, I am prepared to admit that you might have some advantage over the rest of the family, inasmuch as she has never bathed you as an infant or spanked you for stealing raisins from the kitchen. I only hope that I am not precipitating a battle of the Titans."

He tossed the letter into the post-basket.

"I am convinced, Meess Maria that you will not let matters come to such a pass. Moreover..."

He paused.

"I intend to let it be known that I require a steward of the household. I have been remiss in this. When old Papa Mandriano died last winter I hated to put another man in his place. You must understand, Meess Maria, my father was much immersed in politics ... in fact he was imprisoned for his beliefs and I saw little of him when I was a boy. Papa Mandriano looked after his affairs and was a father to me ... he taught me to ride and to shoot and was at my wedding ..."

Mary moved by this picture said nothing. The Paron coughed and frowned at his hands.

"... But sentiment will not collect rents or buy wine," he went on, "and I am to be uncommonly busy this summer. I can't ask too much of you and a steward we must have."

Mary prepared for her descent on the confectioner in the

Calle dei Fabbri with mixed feelings. In her purse was a generous acknowledgement of the services she had done the family since her arrival, which would enable her to repay the Matteos, and to buy Signora Matteo that superb Venetian point-lace cap after which she hankered. It might even stretch to some new clothes for herself which was a pleasant thought. On the other hand, however she might welcome a reduction in her duties, she found herself reluctant to relinquish the reins into other hands. She pinned up her thick golden hair and placed a straw bonnet on top of it.

"If you are not very careful," she told her reflection in the mirror, "you will become a 'femme magistrale' like your Aunt Minerva."

Great Aunt Minerva had kindly but inexorably controlled her vicar husband, her seven children, her husband's parish, her four sons-in-law and anything or anyone else within her orbit, until her premature death at the age of seventy-five of typhus contracted during her determined attempt to control an epidemic in her village. Mary had met this redoubtable relation only once at a very early age, but she had made a lasting impression. She recalled an eagle nose, a frosty blue eye and jutting brows. Anxiously she examined the mirror for Minervan symptoms and happily found none : her eyes were admittedly blue but more mediterranean than arctic in their colour; nor did they tend to pierce people to the bone; her nose was a trifle acquiline but lacked her great-aunt's warhorse quality and her brows, two shades darker than her hair, curved unexceptionably showing no tendency (as yet) to beetle. All in all it was an attractive face, though Mary, accustomed to having it compared with her sister's flower-like countenance, could not be persuaded of this — possibly because she never saw it lit with a gleam of amusement as so many others did.

While Mary was in the confectioners' and restraining Giannina's undisguised greed, Roberto, the Paron's very superior valet, was sipping wine in his usual café and gossiping with his carefully chosen cronies. Within an hour the news that the Muranos required a steward of the household was in every café in Venice. It was not long before it reached a small stuffy office in the Procuratie, where Signor Murano's name had recently come under discussion on more than one occasion. The uniformed occupants of that office received the news with evident excitement and immediately engaged in a round of activities. It would appear that they were, for some reason, anxious to oblige the Paron, for among the many applicants for the post who appeared at the Palazzo the following day was one Paolo Treviso, who had previously been summoned (after dark) to that office, and there furnished with an impressive array of commendations from previous employers whose names he was at some pains to get by heart. He was also provided with a respectable suit of clothes and in deference to Signor Murano's known eccentricities, a bath, a shave and a clean shirt. While he was undergoing this transformation one or two respectable and unemployed Venetians, who had wished to try their luck at the Palazzo, found themselves unaccountably accosted by well-breeched strangers who plied them with wine, so that in the morning they found themselves too ill to attend the interviews. Paolo thus entered the Palazzo with the odds very clearly in his favour; he also had a set of instructions which seemed to have little to do with the duties of a steward.

As none of the other applicants had catered so completely to the tastes of their prospective employer, and Signor Murano could discover no one among the crowd whom he found possible to prefer, Sior Paolo (as he wished to be called) obtained the position. He was introduced into the household by the Paron with a few hurried and conventional phrases before he left for the station and a prolonged journey. It was perhaps unfortunate that the household, individually and collectively, took a marked dislike to Sior Paolo. There seemed no obvious reason for this dislike. Sior Paolo behaved in an exemplary fashion. He was firm, just, decided, friendly, polite, considerate, and (as even Mary had to admit) extremely competent. It would seem that despite his virtues, or possibly even because of them, Sior Paolo was just not likeable. He was a short, flabby man with sharp brown eyes in a pallid, lard-coloured face which seemed always to have a film of sweat upon it. His hair was thin and greasy and his feet tiny like the trotters of a pig. Mary herself found that she had to suppress a degree of hostility, which surprised her, for she was not much given to that emotion. She told herself that it was due to resentment at being supplanted, but this was not precisely true because the household, which unlike herself made no discernible effort to suppress their hostility to the new steward, continued to treat Mary as the Comptroller of the house and consistently and maddeningly referred Sior Paolo's wishes and orders to herself despite all her efforts to abdicate.

It was a curious circumstance that Sior Paolo's impeccable behaviour in the face of such provocation did not make Mary like him any better. He endured pinprick insolence, the contrived and spurious incomprehension, the stupidity and the forgetfulness with a bland good temper which ought to have been admirable : instead it seemed out of character, like a granite outcrop showing through the sward to hint at rock below. It made her uneasy . . . and so did the steward's habit of patrolling the whole house in noiseless list slippers. He seemed to be ubiquitous.

Mary spent the afternoon at the Matteos. When she came back she went straight to the schoolroom. Only Pietro was there, wrestling with the *Pickwick Papers*. When, after an impassioned tribute to English democratic principles, Pietro had consented to learn the English language, Mary had selected the celebrated proceedings of the Pickwick Club as a suitable antidote to his highflown notions of English society. He was now working his bemused way through it with growing fascination. He looked up as she came in and demanded to know at once if the 'hocussing' of electors was a common practice in the town where she was born, and what species of manufacture were 'sarspans' which did not appear in his lexicon and moreover, was that town . . . booroff . . . of Eatanswill now represented by Mr Slumkey of a comparable size to, say, Padua? Mary expounded these and other mysteries of the democratic process and asked where Giannina might be, but while she asked the question she noted that Pietro, usually pale, was flushed and had an air of barely contained excitement; furthermore it did occur to her that the boy had been reading the account of the hustings at Eatanswill the previous week. In fact he had the air of one who had been 'up to something'. Her eye fell on a bulky letter addressed in Pietro's hand lying on the table.

"I've been writing to Alberto," he explained.

Mary looked a little surprised. Brotherly affection was not the most prominent of her pupil's traits. He was more accustomed to refer to Alberto in terms of violent opprobrium than to indite him long letters.

"I . . . we've a notion of a spree," Pietro stammered, "it'll be a famous thing if we can bring it off. I want Alberto to send me something from home . . ."

He flushed more than ever and giggled like a schoolboy.

"Take it down to the post-basket then," said Mary smiling, "I hope you haven't sent for anything which will set your mother all upon end."

Pietro mumbled a disclaimer.

"If you see Giannina send her to me. It's time for her lesson."

Giannina was big with news.

"Meess Maria! She has come!"

"You are late, Giannina," said Mary and struck a chord. "Are you ready?"

"Oh, listen, please. I'll have to get my breath back! I tell you . . . she's come."

"Who has come?"

"Tia Caterina."

"So?"

"Oh, Meess Maria . . . you are *not* stupid. She has heard about you, don't you see?"

Mary nodded.

"I believe your father has informed her that he has engaged another governess."

Giannina came up close to her.

"Tia Caterina rules this family . . . didn't you know?" she

announced. "She isn't just a housekeeper . . . she's a sort of . . . sort of Tsarina. I wager she thinks you are trying to take her place."

She giggled.

"And in a way you have, haven't you?"

"Well, somebody had to take hold and she wasn't here," remarked Mary reasonably.

"Look, you don't understand!" complained Giannina. "She didn't want us to come to Venice in the first place. We haven't been here for two years now and I still don't know why Papa suddenly made up his mind that we should come. I mean it's not as if it was a brilliant society to launch me in, is it? But you see Tia Caterina's second cousin's daughter's married to an Austrian, and this makes it not very nice for her when we're here. People shout things. So she thought if she didn't come Mama would have to do all the things *she* usually does and Papa would be horridly uncomfortable, and we would all have to go back to Monte Colon. But instead *you* came and everything went beautifully and now she's absolutely determined to be rid of you!"

"Is she indeed? And what about you and Pietro? Do you want to be rid of me too?"

"Silly! Would I be telling you all this if we did? Our first English Meess didn't last six weeks."

Mary laughed at this naive admission and then turned back to the piano.

"I don't intend to leave until I want to go . . . or you want me to go. Now . . . please to pay attention to your breathing in bar seven . . ."

"This will be a battle-royal!" said Giannina gleefully.

However, Giannina was to be disappointed. There was no overt battle; in fact there was no battle at all. For this Mary had to thank the fact that Tia Caterina encountered Sior Paolo before she met Mary herself, and being a woman of sense and resource she recognised Mary as an ally in the coming struggle. Tia Caterina did not like Sior Paolo any more than did the rest of the Murano household. Mary found herself drawn into a kind of defensive alliance, because Sior Paolo, recognising in Tia Caterina a truly formidable opponent with none of the scruples which inhibited Mary, moved stealthily on to the offensive. He employed his sharpest weapon, his control of the household expenditure. As soon as Tia Caterina resumed her control of the marketing for the family the household bills were seen to rise sharply. The steward, presenting his weekly accounts made no comment on this circumstance but the inference was plain. Tia Caterina, taken (rather tentatively) to task on this matter by the Paron, took her indignation and frustration to Mary, who evolved a neat scheme. She suggested to the Paron that as both Giannina and Pietro appeared to have inherited their father's head for business, it would be an advantage if they were to be instructed in the mysteries of book-keeping by Sior Paolo. To this end he could use the household accounts as a kind of text-book. Both children entered into this scheme with enthusiasm and accounted with gusto for the expenditure of every soldi. Signor Murano, who had for years winked at a degree of peculation rather than undergo the labour of prevention, sardonically endorsed this masterstroke.

The allies were rather anxiously awaiting Sior Paolo's next move when Angelo, Mary's diminutive cavalier of the cut-down breeches, appeared in the kitchen of the Palazzo with a note. He waited obstinately on the doorstep despite all the blandishments of the kitchen staff, who had long succumbed to his mixture of impertinence and charm, and refused to hand the note to anyone but Mary herself in spite of the attempt by the steward to get him to relinquish it to a silver salver in exchange for a couple of soldi. When Mary came to take it from his own grimy hand, he handed it over with a bow and then accepted an invitation from the Neapolitan cook to sample a bowl of fish soup. The cook approved of Mary and his approval extended to her gondolier friends. Sior Paolo left the scene and Mary opened her letter. She read it once and then went in search of Tia Caterina. It was from Eduardo.

My respected and beloved Miss, [Eduardo began] Do not fear that I renew my importunities. Though I remain constant, I am grateful to a kind fate which has found you a shelter from the chill wind of misfortune which might have driven you to a humbler and less appropriate refuge.

I write to warn you, my cherished Miss, that your bene-factors have admitted a serpent to their bosom. I beg and implore that you should guard your tongues and keep your utterances discreet because P . . . . . . T . . . . . . is *not reliable*. Do not trust him in any matter of *moment*.

Believe me till death your devoted admirer,

Eduardo Torcellano

He had enclosed with this document a card printed in a smudged and uneven fashion which declared its origin. It announced that Eduardo Torcellano 'cellist with many renowned musical ensembles, was now available for public and private engagements and was to be found above Torcellano's Glove Shop in the Mercerie. From this Mary deduced that Eduardo was probably stitching gloves in his brother's workshop.

Tia Caterina was inclined to dismiss that letter as superfluous.

"I would not trust him as far as I could kick him," she told Mary emphatically, "and I don't need that opinion endorsed by any gut-scraper of them all!"

Mary, saving the tart description of poor Eduardo, was inclined to agree with her, but there was another aspect of the matter which she hesitated to mention to the second cousin once removed by marriage to an Austrian.

"Signor Torcellano," she began, "has certain political associations which I will not name. It seems to me that he may wish to convey that Sior Paolo is pro-Austrian by persuasion."

Tia Caterina stared and snorted scornfully.

"Politics!" she ejaculated, "the stupid games that men invent for themselves! As if there weren't trouble enough in the world without politics. Tell young Pietro to keep his sentiments to himself in future or he'll end in jail like his grandfather . . . the moonling. Silly young spitfire. Politics!"

Before Mary could suggest that the Paron be shown the letter when he returned she went away. Mary burned the letter but she did not forget it, though she made no mention of the warning in the little note she despatched to the glove shop.

It was at this point that the Signora Murano unconsciously put an end to the campaign raging through her house by deciding to launch her daughter Giannina into Society with a Grand Ball. That decision taken, there was no time left for hostilities. Balls were scarce in Venice at that time and held on a scale which was so parsimonious as to be positively nasty; but this one promised to be different. A ripple of prosperity emanated from the Palazzo and washed over the flower-sellers, the bakers, the candle-makers, fish-sellers, butchers and poulterers. Further ripples touched the silk merchants and milliners, the shoemakers and mantua-makers, the glovers and the jewellers. Venetian society made up its mind that, for once, there should be an echo of its ancient gaieties. The Palazzo fairly hummed with preparations as the ballroom floor was waxed, and the huge chandeliers washed, lustre by lustre, in soapy water and then charged with hundreds of candles. Gallons of soup were made and mounds of jellies; parcels of favours and baskets of flowers arrived at the door; hundreds of acceptances were delivered by curious servants who informed the Palazzo of their employers' preparations. New servants were hired, old ones were fitted with new liveries, dress-makers, jewellers, hairdressers, dancing-masters and musicians came and went all day. Sior Paolo watched sourly an expenditure on which he could no longer take the customary commission.

Mary helped whenever she was requested by Tia Caterina (which was not more than twice an hour) but spent much of her time making Giannina practise the two songs she was to sing. Her pupil had a true, small, sweet voice but no aptitude whatsoever for any instrument so Mary agreed to play her accompaniment 'on the night'. To that end she bought a demure governess-like tucker of point lace which would furnish forth the blue silk.

On the night of the ball Mary found herself in demand. Her

first duty was to reassure Signora Murano that the new yellow satin gown became her as well as she hoped it did. This was an easy task for the Parona looked her best, her six children and her married son a ridiculous invention. A more arduous task was to persuade Pietro that patriotism did not require him to boycott the proceedings altogether. She was not assisted in these representations by the boy's natural reluctance to expose his gawkiness to public view. She suggested that his new English-style evening clothes were sombre enough to indicate his feelings to those who knew, and persuaded him that there would be so many dancers on the floor that his own shortcomings would be unnoticed. She left him struggling sulkily with his neck-tie.

Outside his door she was way-laid by Marco, who bore a message from Sior Paolo about the placing of the piano in the small salon where the musical part of the evening was to take place. This was settled just as Giannina emerged from her room in a high state of déshabillée and demanding Mary's aid in a disagreement between her and her Mama who, she declared, wanted her to look like a school-girl. The bone of contention was a necklace of garnets left to Giannina by a great-aunt. Mama, who had taken Mary's advice about colour deeply to heart, had had her daughter clad in a cloud of primrose-coloured gauze with which she was supposed to wear a necklace of topaz, single stones strung on a fine chain. Giannina preferred to wear the more spectacular garnets. Mary persuaded her of the folly of detracting from the beauty of eyes and hair set off so admirably by the delicacy of the dress and the jewel. Time enough, she said, to wear the garnets when she wished to distract attention from these. Before she left to get dressed herself the hideous parure was safely locked away.

Mary was still brushing her cloud of fair hair and braiding it into the gleaming chignon she habitually wore, when the first of the guests arrived. Tia Caterina resplendent in shiny black satin and a white lace cap as badge of office tapped on Mary's door.

"From the Parona," she beamed and gave Mary a small box. "Behold!" she exclaimed approvingly when she saw the coil of Venetian chainwork nestling inside. She patted the formidable collection of similar work which draped her own bosom.

"Chain is as good as a dowry to a girl..." she proclaimed and showed Mary how to display it to best advantage on the new lace tucker. She nodded approval of the result.

"The Parona begs that you will attend her in the small salon."

Mary's experience of Venice had not included any formal social occasions such as this. She was thus a trifle taken aback to discover the rigid segregation of the sexes which obtained. The evening was to consist of a musical entertainment in the small salon, a supper generous by any standards and Lucullan by current Venetian ones, and finally dancing in the ballroom. For the first part of this programme she found the salon full of girls firmly chaperoned and displayed to advantage on the chairs and settees, while the male portion of the assembly was penned in the anteroom, able to view the proceedings (and the girls) only through the open double doors. Occasionally a brave soul would venture in to pay his respects to a particular group of ladies, but etiquette forbade more than a brief exchange of civilities and to sit down was a social gaffe of some magnitude. Evidently distance was to lend enchantment to the view and certainly it prevented their discovering the vapidity of the conversation.

Those musical members of the company who had been invited to take part in the concert were grouped around the instruments at the far end. A string ensemble drawn at Mary's suggestion from the orchestra at the Benedetto, now unhappily at leisure to take such evening engagements, waited woodenly nursing their instruments.

The concert dragged a trifle as was inevitable when most of the audience and many of the performers regarded it as a tiresome preliminary to the real business of the evening. Nor did the performers possess talent sufficient to change this view. Only the refreshments handed by Guiseppe and his minions were received enthusiastically.

Giannina's turn came in the second half of the programme. She bounced to her position by the piano, smiled engagingly upon her audience and broke into her songs with an attack which concealed the hours of practice. The Signora smirked maternally at the congratulations which followed, and her husband raised his eyebrows at Mary in a gratifying manner. Giannina collecting her music grinned happily at her accompanist and then her expression changed to one of amusement.

"Here comes my uncle Todaro," she whispered in Mary's ear, "Late as always . . . now you watch all the girls in the room set their caps for him!"

Mary had her back to the double doors and could not see the new arrival but his effect upon the female half of the audience was plain to see. There was a flashing of eyes, an arrangement of profiles and a certain self-consciousness.

"He is a bachelor . . ." hissed Giannina, "and very rich. People say he has sworn never to marry until Venetia is free . . . but . . ."

She shrugged.

"That doesn't seem much in Uncle Todaro's style somehow. I think . . ."

She shuffled the sheets of her music decisively upon the lid of the piano.

". . . I think it's an excuse made up by the Mamas because he doesn't bother with their dear, dull daughters."

Mary laughed at this shrewd observation and wondered, not for the first time, how Signora Murano had produced such a child.

When the music was over and the string orchestra had retired to eat before re-ensembling in the ballroom, the company began slowly to pair off into partners for supper. Mary who had previously arranged to share Tia Caterina's supper in the housekeeper's room remained behind to tidy the music. She was a trifle startled to find her employer advancing upon her with a tall, vaguely familiar figure behind him.

"Signorina, you need no introduction to my graceless brother-in-law," said Signor Murano, "perhaps you would favour him with your company at supper."

Angelo's tall friend bowed and presented his arm. Mary had

opened her mouth to refuse, intending to plead the pressure of her duties, when suddenly she understood who it was had recommended her to the Muranos. She determined to take this chance to thank him. If he was that eligible (if susceptible) Uncle Todaro del Doria, as she suspected he was, she might not have another opportunity. If the raised eyebrows of the Mamas as they entered the supper room were anything to go by, Tia Caterina would have the news of her whereabouts at once.

The opportunity to thank him did not come easily. The eager Mama on his left engaged him instantly and continuously in conversation and he was forced to ignore his partner. The man on Mary's right divided his attention between the delectable scandal being supplied by his own partner and the dainties supplied by his host. Mary resigned herself to silence, sampled the dishes she was offered with a view to complimenting the Neapolitan cook, and observed the work of the servants with a penetrating eye. Marco hastily buttoned the topmost button of his livery and went to change the stained white glove. Guiseppe smiled anxiously and momentarily at her. For the rest of the time she observed the manoeuvres of the girl opposite to attract and hold the attention not of her partner, but of Uncle Todaro. She was smiling at this when the presentation of a dish of meringues released him from the sweet-toothed Mama and he turned to speak to her.

"And what do you find so amusing?" he asked and followed her gaze. The girl was listening to a very dull story from her partner with an attention which would have been excessive in a disciple at the feet of a prophet, eyes shining, lips parted and laugh at the ready.

"Nothing of importance," said Mary hastily and looked down at her plate.

"I have a melancholy suspicion, Signorina, that you derive a good deal of amusement from your fellow-beings."

"No doubt they derive as much from me," she returned and sipped her wine. "Signor, I too have my suspicions."

"Indeed?"

"I suspect you to have imposed upon your brother-in-law a female of whom you could have known very little."

She looked him in the face and found that he was smiling.

"Not that I am ungrateful," she added, "but it seems to me that you took a considerable risk."

He shook his head.

"You do me an injustice. I knew a great deal about you when I wrote that letter."

"Ah, so it *was* you. Now, how could you know the first thing about me after such a brief encounter?"

Guiseppe refilled their glasses.

"Easily," said Uncle Todaro and raised his glass to her," for one thing I knew your politics were as impeccable as your Italian; I also knew you were English by the way you routed the Wachtmeister. I knew you painted in water-colour and painted tolerably well . . ."

He began to check off the points on his fingers.

"You also appeared to have a liking for children and two qualities absolutely essential for a position in this house; an ability to keep your head and to think quickly."

He glanced at her mischievously to see how she appreciated this evaluation of her qualities but she was not listening. Instead she was considering with a rather grim expression the emerald signet-ring of old-fashioned design, which he wore on the little finger of his right hand.

"Nor was this all the information I had about you," he went on smoothly, "I knew of you by hear-say . . ."

He removed the ring and held it between finger and thumb so that she could see the familiar device.

"I had heard of your musical talents for example . . . from, shall we say, a common acquaintance . . ."

"And what impression could she give of my moral qualifications for the instruction of youth?" she asked drily.

"They were the easiest of all to gauge," he said, "that night I had a package from you . . ."

Mary coloured.

"You know," he went on, "I don't think you altogether understood your sister's intentions. She wrote . . ."

He glanced at her and saw a tide of colour invade her face.

". . . she wrote that you were to keep your grandfather's ring. She then added that it was too big for her anyway."

This information replaced the serious look in her eyes with a gleam of amusement.

"Yes, that was Flora," she said appreciatively.

"In the circumstances how could I hesitate to recommend one so sensitive to obligations . . . even those of others."

"I am not sure I understand," said Mary, "I saw no ring and I found no note. Did she write to you?"

"No. She wrote to you," he said and noted her obvious bewilderment, "but I can see how you might not find it. Did it not occur to you that if Flora returned that bauble, I might expect her also to return certain others?"

By this time the company was draining glasses and preparing to remove to the ballroom. The Mama on del Doria's left was waiting impatiently for an opportunity to regain his attention. With a kind of shocked incredulity she saw her quarry take his most unsuitable partner's hand and put a ring on the finger. All down the table conversations died and heads turned.

"She omitted to mention that it was also too big for you," he observed.

She took it off and put it in her reticule.

"I had better keep it till I . . ."

"Until when?" he asked mischievously, "until you grow up?"

Mary choked back a laugh.

"Signor," she told him reproachfully, "my height is no subject for jesting. I was going to say until I grow fat."

He rose to his feet and pulled out her chair.

"An unlikely eventuality in this house. Give it to me and I will have it made to fit you."

She shook her head and walked ahead of him, while the company speculated and gossiped and recalled his spectacular liaison with another Miss Porretuse . . .

The string orchestra, much refreshed by a square meal, played the waltzes and quadrilles with an enthusiasm echoed by the dancers. Segregation, however, remained the rule. The chaperones sat along one wall watching their charges like Argus himself and no delay in returning a partner to their care after the music had ended was tolerated. The men congregated on the other side of the room eyeing the girls and waiting for the music to begin so that they might claim their choices, or retreated into the anteroom to smoke their long cigars and talk politics. Among the latter was del Doria who had danced a country dance with his niece and a waltz with her governess before retiring. Mary appreciated the opportunity to dance, but would have preferred obscurity to the spiteful attention his action drew upon her from the frustrated Mamas and their charges. Nor did any other gentleman follow del Doria's example, for which she was not ungrateful as none of them could look comfortably over her shoulder. She found a chair in a darkish corner and sat down to wait until the evening should be over.

However, this retreat was invaded by Signora Murano who begged that she should take charge of Giannina while the Signora refreshed herself with a game of parchesi. Mary professed herself happy to oblige and with this lie on her lips, removed to a seat among the chaperones from which she could observe Giannina. She found her person under discussion and her character under attack and if this ceased when she arrived, neither the chaperones nor their charges so much as acknowledged her existence, let alone her presence.

It was perhaps in an attempt to relieve this ostracisation that Signor Murano brought the American consul, Mr Howells, and his wife over to meet her. This move was not a success. Mr Howells was a Yankee who had grown up with the Liberty Bell ringing in his ears and learned his letters from heroic tales of Paul Revere and the Boston Tea Party. Mr Howells did not care for the British though he was scrupulous in admitting their virtues, and he was sufficient of a Brahmin not to appreciate being introduced to a mere governess in such elevated society, be she never so Anglo-Saxon. His wife, a pretty little robin of a woman was prepared to be friendly with anyone who would speak her mother-tongue, however alien the accent, but she took her colour from her husband. Dean Howells was a little too consciously democratic and Mary a little too plainly amused by this.

"And how do you go on in Venice?" Mary enquired of Mrs Howells, "Do you find the dialect very difficult?"

"My wife has the distinction of speaking less Italian every week she spends here," said the Consul, "it is quite remarkable."

This observation effectively ended his wife's attempts to make conversation and shortly afterwards they took their leave while there was an interval in the dancing.

The absence of the orchestra presented an opportunity for more of the female guests to display their accomplishments and the company, mellowed by food and wine, were readier to appreciate them. Mary was pressed into service as an accompanist. She had just succeeded in following a wandering contralto through an idiosyncratic version of Handel and was receiving her sotto voce criticisms in polite silence, when one of the older women who had observed sourly Mary's earlier dealings with del Doria, rustled across and tapped her on the shoulder imperiously.

"Ah, Signorina Porretuse... I wish you would settle an argument."

"If I can, Signora," said Mary.

"They say that you were a singer at the Benedetto before you were employed here. Is this true?"

"No, Signora. I did not sing there."

"No? But there was a Porretuse at the Benedetto. It was well known."

The woman sneered.

"So was she," she added.

"My sister, Signora."

"My friends have confused you with her, no doubt?"

Mary raised her eyebrows.

"Are they very shortsighted, your friends?" she enquired solicitously. "We are not at all alike."

There was a flutter of amusement at this counterstroke, and the woman reddened.

"You overestimate our interest in the matter." she snapped, "Such people are known to us only by reputation . . . or lack of it."

Mary went a little pale. Signora Murano with the true hostess's instinct for a contretemps, had returned from the cardroom in time to hear most of the exchange, broke the silence which greeted this remark.

"But my dear Maria," she exclaimed, a mode of address which defined precisely the position which Mary held in her esteem, "you are far too modest. I was daring to hope that you might sing for us tonight."

"But Signora, I . . ."

Giannina came quickly to her governess's side.

"Take no notice of old lemon-face," she whispered, none too quietly, "she's been after Uncle Todaro for years for that dumpling-faced daughter of hers . . . and he doesn't even remember her name . . ."

Fans were placed over mouths to hide smiles and the woman stiffened with anger at the half-caught words.

"Giannina, behave," said Mary.

Giannina watched the retreating figure of Mary's opponent.

"Pietro's promised me to deal with her," she confided, "he's going to ask her to dance the waltz and then tread all over her feet !"

At such incontrovertible evidence of trust and esteem Mary's anger died and she would dearly have liked to laugh. Instead she nodded at Giannina and played the introduction to an impertinent little folk tune from the Abruzzi which they had been used to singing as a duet. Giannina, flown with excitement and admiration, joined in with a will and the unpleasantness was soon forgotten. The woman finding herself a little unpopular later went home to bathe her feet.

Uncle Todaro who had been observing events in the ballroom as he smoked and chatted in the anteroom strolled in shortly after midnight to make his adieux. He bowed gracefully over his sister's hand, then made an elaborate burlesque of a 'pretendant' begging for a kiss from his beautiful niece, which reduced her to helpless giggles and roused the most unworthy feelings in the breasts of all the young guests who witnessed it. The kiss achieved he turned suddenly to Mary who was watching the pantomime highly entertained by both players and audience.

"Signorina," he said and took her hand.

She saw that his mischievous expression had vanished and that he was looking across at the orchestra.

"Behold," he said softly, "can you tell me how long my nephew has been acquainted with *him*?"

Pietro was talking in an elaborately casual manner to Cesare Galeffi, the viola player.

"I cannot say," replied Mary, very conscious of her hand in his. "I should think only tonight..."

"I devoutly hope you are right."

He kissed her hand briefly, smiled, bowed and was gone.

5

"What a jest, what a jape!"

Um Ballo in Maschera: VERDI

THE MURANO'S BALL SEEMED to release a spring of hospitality long suppressed. Those who had restricted their entertaining in support of the Dimostrazione suddenly discovered that their guest lists could be used as weapons in the long struggle. Anyone who frequented the Austrian cafés, who strolled in the Piazza while the Austrian military bands played themes from the opera (a temptation hard to resist for any Venetian), or who was seen to speak with an Austrian on whatever pretext, these found that they were left off the guest lists and had to sit alone in the café while their friends frolicked elsewhere. One hostess with a particular hatred of the occupying power restricted her guests to those who had done some open act of defiance. As she kept an uncommonly good table, something rare in Venice, there was a rash of anti-Austrian impudences. Pamphlets appeared everywhere, especially in the Austrian cafés, posters bloomed on the calle walls, local composers brought out impertinent songs which were sung by the lasagnoni as the soldiers marched past, the words just loud enough for the soldiers to realise their nature without being able to distinguish their sense. The girls of Venice turned their backs on the garrison, and the few who did not, found themselves unpopular with their regular clientele and a few were jostled into an ignominious ducking. Anyone who looked like an Austrian found walking in the city an uncomfortable experience.

The Muranos shared fully in this revival of hospitality. Some three weeks after their own ball they were invited to attend another. However, Signora Murano discovering that her prospective hostess did not intend to provide a cardroom, found

herself quite prostrated by her recent exertions and asked that
Mary would deputise for her. Thus it was that on the evening
of the ball only Giannina and Mary boarded Alessandro's
gondola. He and Angelo by methods understood to themselves
alone, had constituted theirs the official craft for the Palazzo
Murano. Alessandro, who had swiftly assumed the status of
privileged family retainer, commented ecstatically upon their
appearance. They directed him to the Campo Santa Maria
Formosa where they disembarked and asked that he would take
them up again around half past eleven. He waved assent and
vanished into the press of boats upon this busy canal. It was
not until he had gone that Mary noticed that the Palazzo to
which they were bidden was unlit and unwelcoming. On the
broad green-stained marble steps stood a dumpy figure dressed
all in black, his head bent in an attitude of mourning like the
statues made to stand on Italian tombs. Puzzled by this Mary
accosted him. He raised his drooping head.

"Your pardon, Signorinas, but my mistress requests that I
inform you that there will be no ball held here tonight. It was
hoped that all the guests would be advised of this before they
left but time did not permit."

He shook his head lugubriously.

"May one enquire why?" asked Mary, uncertain whether to
be alarmed or annoyed.

Their informant removed his hat, generously wound in black
crepe, and held it against his heart.

"My master the Count," he explained," and it gives me
profound distress to tell you this, my poor master this afternoon
ascended to his chamber and laid down upon his bed to rest
himself before taking his part in the evening's festivities. At five
minutes to six o'clock his valet, devoted man . . ."

He blew his nose upon a black-edged kerchief and wiped his
eyes.

". . . his valet entered and found that our dear master was
dead."

He paused and again shook his head.

"We have such treasures on all too short a lease," he commented.

Mary who knew something of the deceased felt that this was a slight exaggeration but forebore to mention it.

"His health has been fragile . . . though none suspected how fragile," the man continued. "Alas, his loss will be felt."

He bowed his head.

"Convey our condolences to the Contessa," said Mary with appropriate solemnity, "Signora Murano will be distressed beyond measure."

The servant bowed his acknowledgment of this and resumed his hat and the lachrymose attitude in which they had found him. It was quite plain that his grief was tempered by enjoyment of his role. Mary and Giannina, sobered by this sharp reminder of mortality, withdrew to the well-head in the Campo.

"Poor Elena . . ." said Giannina, referring to the daughter of the household, "what a terrible shock it must have been . . ."

Mary agreed, rather absentmindedly because she was a little distressed by the predicament in which they found themselves. Girls and young women did not walk about Venice at night without male escort. For herself she did not mind, but Giannina could be exposed to the kind of comment and attentions which every gently bred female ought to dislike, and while Giannina was more likely to giggle than to swoon at the gallantries it was, none the less, not what her mother would wish to happen. The knot of gondolas usually to be found waiting for custom at the bridge was not there. Either previous arrivals at the Palazzo had engaged them or it was dinner hour for the boatmen.

"We will find a boat at the Ponte di Paglia," decided Mary.

The way to the Piazza was longer than that to the Rialto but it was better lit and more frequented. She took Giannina's hand and tucked it in her arm.

"Pull the hood of your cloak well over your face," she advised, "and take no notice of anybody no matter what they may say."

They set out at a fair pace, Giannina pattering along to keep up with Mary's long stride, her gauze skirts held in her hand. They were passing under the Clocktower when they came face to face with Pietro who also appeared to be in a hurry. Giannina greeted him with a squeal of surprise for he had declared his virtuous intention of keeping their mother company that night instead of going with them as he had been pressed to do.

"And what are you doing here?" Giannina demanded. "Has Mama decided to walk in the Piazza all of a sudden?"

As the Parona never in any circumstances walked anywhere this sally passed for a joke at which Pietro smiled rather wrily.

"Mama retired early to her room," he explained, "I suggested that she might be more comfortable ..."

He suddenly realised that his sister's presence required as much, if not more, explanation as his own.

"... and why are you not dancing your slippers through at Elena's?"

"You meant that if she went to bed you'd be able to come out and gad about," accused his sister.

Mary ended the incipient quarrel.

"Never mind why he is here. It's a stroke of good fortune for us whatever the reason."

She explained what had happened in a few words.

"... I am sure you will be good enough to escort your sister home," she told him in a manner which left him in no doubt of the required response.

"But I ... that is can you not ... I am with friends ..." he protested.

For the first time Mary noticed that he made one of a group and a group, moreover, which seemed uncommonly anxious to be on their way, for they were edging their way round in an attempt to reach the entrance to the calle on their left. One of them carried a large and apparently heavy bundle which he clutched feverishly as if it might escape his grasp. Another was wearing a wide-brimmed hat pulled well down over his face, but Mary was well-acquainted with the tubby figure and the greenish-black cloak which covered it.

"Signor Torcellano," she exclaimed with pleasure, "may I trespass upon your good nature and request your company as far as the Ponte di Paglia."

Eduardo stammered out his pleasure at such a prospect but he looked apprehensively at the fourth member of the group, a much younger man. Mary recognised in him the viola player who had joined the orchestra at the Benedetto on the day of the riot.

"No," said the fourth man and he had a ring of authority in his voice. "I need you, Eduardo . . . Signorina . . ."

He turned to Mary and Giannina.

"I crave your indulgence, Signorinas, but this is no idle excursion . . . we have an appointment. An appointment of some importance . . ."

An agonised exclamation escaped from the member of the party who was carrying the blanket-wrapped bundle, and it seemed to Mary that the bundle gave a convulsive wriggle.

". . . an appointment," Cesare continued smoothly, "which we cannot possibly postpone. I urgently need Signor Torcellano's presence. Pietro may go with you . . . his part is played."

He turned to Eduardo and said in an urgent undervoice not meant for Mary's sharp ears.

"Don't be a fool . . . only you know the way in."

Eduardo made a gesture of regret and apology.

"Meess!" he exclaimed, "I am damnably placed. It distresses me beyond measure to disoblige . . ."

As Mary opened her mouth to beg him not to distress himself he was plucked out of sight by Cesare and the three vanished from sight into a narrow passageway. Pietro left thus unceremoniously looked anything but pleased. He glared at his sister and her companion and looked as if he would have consigned them to the escort of Old Nick himself if that worthy had appeared and made the offer. He seemed on the verge of bursting into angry protest and restrained himself only when a curious sound echoed from the passageway, a kind of hoarse and muffled squealing. Pietro looked alarmed and turned quickly to his companions holding out an arm to each.

"Come then!" he said with a very bad grace and they emerged into the Piazza under his escort.

It was a sufficiently beautiful sight in the afterglow of sunset and with a galaxy of lamps and candles illuminating the cafés.

The Specchi where the Italianissimi congregated was lit entirely by candles and the atmosphere (fittingly enough) seemed almost conspiratorial. Certainly it was not possible to recognise the faces of those who sat at the tables. The musicians inside the café dispensed their version of Italian opera music quietly and almost automatically as if they were straining their ears to hear the schemes which were being hatched around the pink-shaded candles on each table : and the system of espionage being what it was, it was entirely possible that at least one of them was trying to do just that. The dark clothes and subdued manners of the customers lent colour to this illusion of conspiracy though, as the subject of conversation at every table ranged monotonously round the same painful political subject the lowered voices and precautionary glances were only sensible; at all events they appeared so at the beginning of the conversation. Later as feelings began to run high in a passion of mutual agreement such precautions were forgotten. In the circumstances it was, perhaps, just as well that the whole width of the Piazza divided them from the Quadri. The Quadri was the principal resort of the Austrian officers of the garrison and such Venetians as consorted with them. The Quadri was more opulently lit than the Specchi, having eight lamps suspended from the striped canopy which sheltered the tables set outside and three chandeliers inside, all ablaze with candles. The company thus illuminated, resplendent in white uniforms, gold lace and glittering buttons made a marked contrast with the sombrely dressed civilians across the square. Moreover, the waiters waited with more aplomb and less desperation than they did in the Specchi (possibly because they could see what they were doing, which was more than could the staff at the Specchi). The music from the Quadri was predominantly German, Wagner being a prime favourite as that composer had noted with complacence on his recent visit to the city, and dispensed with an appropriate fortissimo.

Mary, Giannina and their conscripted escort did not at first pause to admire this very Venetian scene, but before they were halfway across the great square the clock struck and Giannina wriggled her arm out of her brother's and turned about to watch the Moors striking on the bell, a sight which gave her a childish pleasure. Pietro looked longingly at the busy cafés.

"Would you object," he said awkwardly, looking at Mary, "if we were to try for a boat at the Pontili San Marco. The Riva is covered with sleeping lasagnoni at this hour. Not a place for you and Nina at all."

Mary knew this to be true and she was glad to escape the cloud of beggars which lurked about the landing stages beyond the Piazzetta. Unescorted she would not have taken Giannina the length of the Piazza but with Pietro there could be no objection. They gathered up their skirts, adjusted the hoods of their cloaks and taking the arms offered by Pietro, joined the crowd which jauntered aimlessly across the marble flags between the noisy cafés. At first Mary tried to make Pietro walk a little faster but he refused.

"Surely you do not wish to be conspicuous?" he said smugly and reprovingly and continued to stroll at the dawdling pace of those about them.

Mary found his attitude a little troubling, but she was in truth unwilling to draw attention to Giannina's reprehensible presence, so she acquiesced though not without wondering just what Pietro was about. Giannina her hood gradually slipping back stared around her at the new and excitingly illicit after-dark world of the city. All about them the young bloods of Venice chattered, smoked their long thin cigars and loudly planned the next onslaught upon the virtue of their latest inamoratas. Above the stir, the music, the clatter of china and glass and the chatter, pigeons roosted on every ledge. Pietro walked more and more slowly as they came to the centre of the Piazza and Mary noticed that his eyes were fixed upon the brilliant scene under the striped canopy of the Quadri; she wondered at this, expecting him to look for acquaintances among the patrons of Specchi's.

Suddenly there was a shrill, ear-splitting squealing from the Austrian café, a din so piercing that the roosting pigeons rose with a clatter of wings. The overture to *Lohengrin* ceased abruptly with an agonised cry from the violinist, as he was hurled off the little platform where he and his companions were playing apparently by his chair, which seemed to have developed a malevolent life of its own, for it leaped down from the platform and crashed into the nearest table, knocking over bottles and glasses full and empty, so that the customers at that table jumped up cursing in German and dabbing at the red wine-stains on their white uniforms with the cloth nearest to hand. It was unfortunate that two of them grabbed the tablecloth at the same time for this purpose and sent the glasses and bottles crashing to the ground where the latter, rolling underfoot, brought down a scurrying waiter and his high-held tray which was laden with scalding knödelsuppe for a homesick party in the far corner. This delicacy, greasy and thick with succulent scraps of pork and savoury doughballs, was showered upon the very senior officer at yet another table, who was entertaining a bedizened female to champagne and meringues with a view to being entertained by her later in the evening. The scream she gave as she was hit on the bosom by a soup-bowl was drowned by his bellow as his bald head (being in close proximity to that bosom) was dowsed in the contents.

The strollers in the Piazza were stopped in their tracks by these portents and stared open-mouthed at the comet-trail of chaos which seemed to be sweeping through the café. One table after another was overturned or the startled occupants pitched out of their chairs by some unseen agent. Another waiter with a trayload of opened bottles found himself suddenly charged by a table which felled him to the ground scattering his bottles over a wide selection of the occupying forces. A customer on the outside standing up to discover what caused these catastrophes felt a body charge between his legs, lost his balance and fell upon that body; he was carried willy-nilly a few yards into the Piazza to the bewilderment of the people watching until he managed to disentangle himself from his mysterious steed. Only then could the author of all the disturbance be clearly seen; he ran hither and thither his trotters rattling on the marble and squealing like a soul in torment.

The invader of the Quadri was a small pig clad in blue

uniform trousers and white tunic laced with gold. A hole had been cut to permit the appearance of his expressive tail, tight-curled with panic. At one time someone had tried to attach the high cap of an Austrian soldier to his head, but his exertions in the café had resulted in its now hanging under his jaw like an exotic dewlap. By the time he appeared he was a very battered, bruised and bewildered pig; he plunged first one way and then another at the ring of onlookers, the majority of whom were now helpless with laughter before vanishing out of the light and out of this tale between the two great columns in the Piazzetta ... though his fate, Venice being a hungry city, was not really in doubt.

He left behind a confusion of overturned chairs, tables, patrons and staff in the Quadri and hilarious delight among the watching crowd. The patrons of the Specchi caused nearly as much damage to the furniture of their own chosen venue by jumping upon the chairs and tables to watch the scene and to cheer 'Il Generale Porco'.

Mary, Giannina and Pietro found themselves wedged in the centre of the crowd who were jeering at the Austrians picking themselves up out of the welter of broken glass, spilt wine and broken meats.

"Come," said a voice in Mary's ear, "let us remove from here before the Whites come around and ask questions."

She found her arm taken by Eduardo, who elbowed a passage for her to the supportega into the Calle di Acenzione, while Pietro recalled to a sense of his responsibilities, did the same for Giannina. At the Pontili San Marco they found a waiting gondola whose proprietor had heard the uproar and was consumed with curiosity. He listened to Pietro's racy account of the affair in the Quadri with the closest attention, which made their course along the Canalazzo dangerously erratic. At the Palazzo steps he held the boat alongside while emitting deep, hoarse chuckles.

"Should I see him I will give him free passage to Mestre," he declared as Pietro handed his sister out and Eduardo offered his arm to Mary.

"See whom?" asked Eduardo distractedly as the boatman in his delight had let the gunwale drift away from the steps and he found himself bestriding the waters like a plump Colossus of Rhodes.

"A pig in uniform, Signor!" he cried redressing this mishap.

"But," called Pietro from the top of the steps just as the door opened, "the whole city is full of pigs in uniform. How will you choose?"

He threw a coin at the boatman whose vociferous delight at this sally did not affect his ability to catch coin in midflight, an ability marked in the Venetian for whom a coin missed was a coin lost for ever. Sior Paolo who, in the absence of Guiseppe, who had taken his old bones to bed, decided to open the door himself seemed less taken with the jest. His face was expressionless as he held the door and bowed the party inside, but it seemed to Mary that he peered at the departing Eduardo with an unjustified interest.

Upstairs Mary caught Pietro by the arm as he made to go into his room.

"I have to thank you, Pietro. I was sorry to spoil your evening with your friends . . ."

He muttered a disclaimer but Mary ignored this and looked him in the eye.

". . . if," she added, "it was in fact spoiled."

He tried to pull away but Mary kept her hand where it was.

"Tell me," she enquired, "did Alberto send you what you wanted from Monte Colon?"

Pietro flushed to the roots of his hair and dived into his bedroom.

It was not long before Mary had another hint that Pietro's political sympathies might be having a practical expression.

When the hot weather came Mary found herself employed more and more as a chaperone. Lessons began in the cool of the morning and ceased before midday. A light meal was followed by a somnolent interlude, after which the Muranos joined their fellow Venetians outside. Alessandro would take them to shop in the Mercerie or in the more recherché establishments near the Piazza. They might then stroll in the public gardens or attend a mass or visit friends. Occasionally the Signora went with them, more often she remained at home on her daybed recruiting her energies for the evening's gaieties while Mary chaperoned Giannina. On occasion Pietro could be persuaded to join them.

He was with them on one afternoon in June when Giannina went to choose a wedding present for a friend. This choice had involved much heart-searching for, as Giannina said, it was far more difficult to choose a present for a person one did not much care for. So many considerations came into play which had little to do with generosity. After much argument and some sharp bargaining, the party settled upon a set of goblets in ruby-coloured glass and gilt which Mary privately condemned as hideous. This transaction complete, they strolled across the Piazza and made for the Riva degli Schiavoni where Alessandro was to wait for them. Pietro greeted a group of his friends in Florian's and paused to chat while Mary and Giannina watched the Moors beating upon the bell on the Clocktower. Suddenly, the crowd about them surged uncomfortably and Mary felt herself jostled and pushed; a man elbowed his way past, his head screwed over his shoulder and vanished round the corner of San Marco breaking into a run as soon as he was out of the sunshine.

"Well, really!" said Giannina indignantly clutching the goblets to her.

Mary was frowning as she watched Pietro strolling towards them between two of his cronies; was it or was it not intentional that the three should be in the way of two white-uniformed figures who were evidently in pursuit of the unmannerly gentle-man. They pushed past at last and ignoring the ironical and over-polite apologies of the trio made off round the corner of the Cathedral.

"What was it?" Giannina demanded.

"Only a matter of some pamphlets upon the tables at Florian's" replied Pietro casually, but with a note of triumph, "I was lucky enough to secure one."

He produced it. It was much the same as most of the others

Mary had seen from time to time. It appealed to the populace to resist the enemy, to harass him, to have nothing to do with him; it assured them of the sympathy of all right-minded peoples and of the support of Free Italy. In a passage which could only be described as purple, it promised a Day Which Would Certainly Come when the soil of Mother Italy would be freed from the contamination carried by the foot of the invader. . . . There was something about the style which Mary found familiar.

"The Comitato have recruited a new writer, I see," she observed drily and looked at Pietro who confirmed her suspicion by blushing scarlet and snatching the paper from her. Giannina clapped her hands to her mouth and giggled.

"No such thing!" snapped Pietro and led the way to the Ponte di Paglia at a great rate.

Once in Alessandro's gondola and out on the waters of the Canalazzo the sun struck strongly into their eyes. Mary, whose fair skin reddened painfully in the sun, raised her parasol and opened it to shade her face. To her astonishment, her companions and the whole boat were showered with papers. She picked one up and saw the familiar smudged type and faulty setting of the pamphlet she had read in the Piazza. Pietro's face was a study in exasperation and dismay.

"He must have dropped them in your sunshade!" he exclaimed, "What a dastardly thing! If the Whites had found them . . . what then?"

Giannina began to laugh and he turned on her.

"Suppose Meess Maria had opened it in the Piazza?" he insisted. "She could be in jail by now!"

"No sense in speculation," said Mary calmly and began to gather up the scattered sheets. "The present question is how we may safely dispose of these?"

"Leave that to me," offered Pietro, "I can . . ."

Mary frowned at him.

"Can you indeed?" she commented, "I believe I would prefer to deal with them myself."

"I'm not a child!" exclaimed the boy angrily and Giannina looked from one to the other in bewilderment.

"It would be no use to suggest that you are playing with fire?" Mary returned quietly.

"None in the world!"

"In that case . . ."

She handed him the bundle and he stowed it safely away.

"What is all this about?" demanded Giannina.

The boat bumped gently against the landing stage at the Palazzo Murano.

"I have a mournful premonition," said Mary, gathering her skirts in her hand, "that you may well find out before too long."

Pietro jumped out on to the platform and held out his hand.

"Believe me, I'll try to prevent that as long as I can," he promised.

Mary looked at him and sighed before she turned away to settle with Alessandro. She tried to frame the words in her mind with which she would warn the Paron that his son was playing with fire and that he was, moreover, a very poor conspirator. She was to find quite soon that she had an unexpected and powerful ally in this project.

If the Muranos had been deprived of one ball by the untimely demise of the host there had been invitations to others. One of these was to a function to be held some three days after the episode of the pamphlets. Rather to Mary's surprise Pietro readily agreed to go with his mother and sister in his father's room. Even more to her surprise Mary herself was included in the invitation, though she knew this to be a political gesture rather than a defiance of social usage, as England was currently regarded as a bastion of freedom. She had been allowed to decline only after a prolonged argument with Giannina.

"You won't need me there . . . your mother will be with you and your aunt . . ."

The Parona's sister had appeared in Venice, her meek husband bobbing in her wake. She it was who restricted her guest-lists to the active Italianissimi.

"They don't see the funny things the way you do," pouted Giannina.

"Such as pigs in uniform?" asked Mary.

"Please come, Meess Maria . . . you ought to enjoy yourself sometimes. Not always be the governess."

"Dear girl, you may not believe this but balls are not my notion of enjoyment."

"Why not?"

"Because no one ever asks me to dance. I am so tall that every partner thinks I am a caryatid . . . they're frightened that if they tempt me to move from my place by the wall the roof will fall in."

"What nonsense you talk!" cried Giannina, "And anyway it is not so at all. Uncle Todaro will dance with you."

Mary would not allow this to be a temptation.

On the evening of the ball she saw the trio off in the care of Alessandro and Angelo. She retired to her room to make ready for a visit to the Matteos with whom she planned to eat supper and afterwards to visit the Marionette Theatre. She was still in her petticoats when Tia Caterina tapped on her door.

"Meess Maria, one wishes to see you."

Her expression was a mixture of admiration and disapproval. Mary stopped brushing her hair and stared.

"Who?"

"Signor del Doria."

"It will be the Paron he has called to see."

"He is with the Paron but he has asked to see you."

Mary turned back to the mirror and frowned at her reflection in the glass.

"I will come as soon as I am ready," she said.

When she entered the Paron's study del Doria was alone.

"My brother-in-law discovered an appointment," he explained and considered Mary's bonnet and gloves, "and so have you, it would seem.

Mary explained her plans for the evening.

"Is that Enrico Matteo, the bass?"

"Yes. We had lodgings in . . . but you know, of course."

"I do." he admitted and picked up his broad-brimmed hat, "May I go with you? I want to have a word in your ear and a walk would be more discreet than a tête à tête here in this house . . ."

"If you like."

Guiseppe opened the side door for them and they strolled across the Campo San Pantalon in the soft lamplight.

"Are you not attending the Cornaros' ball?" asked Mary.

"I was invited. As were you," he observed, "I was hoping to see you there, as a matter of fact."

Mary wondered briefly how he had learned of her decision not to go, and what it was he wanted to say to her. Just as he was about to begin his explanation they were accosted by a seller of straw hats who, seeing Mary's height and appearance, mistook them for tourists; a few soft idiomatic sentences from del Doria exposed this for a delusion but within a few hundred yards a cake-seller, a flower-woman and a pedlar of beads were all similarly mistaken, and the reason for del Doria's wishing to speak with her was still a mystery.

As they crossed the bridge over the Rio di San Polo he began "I was wondering if my . . ."

And he was interrupted by a beggar in a strategic position on the steps of the bridge, who gently but persistently pressed his claim to their charity in a mixture of English and German. Del Doria flung him a couple of coins and taking Mary by the arm hurried her down on to the fondamente.

"Barca! Barca!" he called. "We'll take a gondola to the Calle di Fuseri. It's the only way we will have peace to talk."

Once in the little craft threading their way out on to the Grand Canal with the gondolier accompanying his rowing with a song they could talk quietly.

"It's about Pietro," he explained at last, "what does my brother-in-law intend to do with that boy?"

"I don't know. I wish I did. I don't think Pietro knows either. He wants to go to the university at Padua or spend a year in England."

"He's bored and restless. It's not good for him. And it worries me; he ought to have some occupation at his age and not be kept dangling at his mother's skirts."

"I agree with you," said Mary. "Did you ask Signor Murano himself?"

"I did," said del Doria, "and he told me it was no business of mine. When I pressed the matter he discovered this appointment of his. You know Antonio the oldest boy, the one who is married? He's quiet enough now but when he was at the University in Padua he was involved with a very radical group and was put in prison. In fact he was nearly executed for subversion ..."

"I understand now," said Mary. "He's afraid the same thing could happen to Pietro."

Del Doria gave a short laugh.

"I think he's too late. Did you hear about the pig in uniform?" he asked.

It was Mary's turn to chuckle.

"Hear about it! Signor, we were there!"

She recounted the history of the military pig, wondering a little that he did not appear to share her amusement at the ridiculous episode.

"And what is more," she concluded, "I have a distinct suspicion that the pig came from Monte Colon."

He looked at her approvingly.

"You seem to keep your eyes open."

He frowned.

"Just the same, I don't have to tell you how serious the consequences of this could be."

"Serious consequences? But surely ... a silly practical joke like that ..."

"Serious enough."

He looked unexpectedly grim.

"I don't want to see my nephew shot or hanged."

Mary felt as if she had swallowed a lump of ice.

"But they wouldn't ... they couldn't ..."

"My dear Meess Porretuse ... where do you think they laid hold of that uniform?" he asked her. "That same night they found an Austrian soldier dead in the Rio San Vio. He'd been killed by a blow on the neck and his uniform stripped off him."

Mary swallowed.

"You mean that someone killed him for the uniform?"

"It would appear so," agreed her companion gravely.

"But Pietro ... he couldn't ..."

"If he didn't do it he's in a string with the people who did."

"But what sort of people would do that?" demanded Mary angrily, "I mean ... no one likes the Austrians being here but they do no harm. They don't bully anyone ... or anything like that ..."

"Not yet," agreed del Doria, "but there is a group of people in the city now who might force them to behave more like an army of occupation ... who want them to do so."

"Who?"

"They call themselves the Young Carbonari, after Garibaldi's followers ten years ago. We know roughly who they are ... and I would not be surprised if the Austrians know who they are too. And Pietro's been running tame with them ever since the family arrived in Venice."

"What sort of people can they be?"

Del Doria shrugged.

"It is hard to say. They are youngsters for the most part. Some of them are hot-heads imported from Free Italy who think that the Comitato is not doing enough to be rid of the Austrians. They think the methods of ostracisation and ridicule are too tame. They intend to use other methods and the Comitato will find it difficult either to stop them or to dissociate itself from them."

"Methods like murder?" asked Mary.

"They don't regard it as murder," said del Doria sardonically, "they call it war ... a more honourable description of killing. Unfortunately the Austrians are unlikely to see it in the same light. The killers will be hanged when ... if ... they are caught."

Mary felt sick. She remembered Eduardo's evident fear of the young viola player and by an association of ideas she thought of Sior Paolo. If Pietro were as involved as his uncle appeared to believe, Sior Paolo's 'reliability' became a matter of acute importance and his presence in the house a real threat. She told del Doria about Eduardo's letter and he nodded.

"I should think he's after the father, not the son."

Mary gasped.

"You cannot be serious."

Del Doria laughed at her.

"It seems that my brother-in-law is a better actor than I took him for. Have you not discovered that he is an important member of the Comitato?" he explained. "He is our link with the Italian government. Paolo is an Austrian spy. We know this."

"But," protested Mary, "doesn't the Paron understand about Pietro and these people . . . he simply cannot be discreet, Pietro, he gives himself away with every sentence. Haven't you told him this?"

"I have tried," he said, "but my brother-in-law is a man of fixed opinions. He refuses to think that the Young Carbonari should be taken seriously or that Pietro's association with them is a matter for worry. He laughed at the idea."

Mary clasped her hands in her lap.

"I've tried to make Pietro hold his tongue . . . ever since I had that letter . . . but you know what he is. Sior Paolo cannot but surmise he's up to something and before long he is bound to find proof. Pietro is so thoughtless."

"Don't worry too much. Sior Paolo may well ignore the sprat in order to hook the big fish."

"I take it the Paron knows about Sior Paolo," she suggested.

"Oh, yes."

"And does Sior Paolo realise that he is . . . discovered . . ."

Mary laughed and expanded her question.

"I mean does he know that the Paron knows."

Del Doria shook his head.

"No, he believes himself undetected," he announced solemnly but his eyes twinkled, "It was one of our friends in the Procuratie who saw him and reported to us. We too have our agents, you know."

"But why does the Paron not dismiss him?"

"You have a saying in English, I believe, 'better the devil you know . . .' The Government are bound to try to put a spy in the household; it's as well to know who it is."

"It's a fearful coil," observed Mary, "tell me, how can I help?"

"Try to persuade my brother-in-law that Pietro ought to go to England to complete his education. He might listen to you. He has a great respect for your judgment, he told me so. And in the meanwhile keep your eyes open . . . wide open. Let me know at once if you think he may be in trouble. If he doesn't come home one night, for example . . . or if he gets arrested. I might be able to help."

The gondolier let out a wild yell which indicated his intention to turn right handed under the Riva del Carbon and into the narrow canal which crossed the Calle di Fuseri. Del Doria pulled out a card from his pocket and gave it to her.

"That is where my lodging is," he told her, "send a message there if there is need."

"You think there might be need?"

He stood up ready to hand her ashore. By the dim light of the lamp burning in the shrine on the corner his face looked rather grim.

"I have a notion the young fools have got their hands on something more dangerous than a pig."

He escorted her to the Matteos' door and was there hospitably drawn inside and fed lavishly upon fish soup, risotto with peppers and zabaglione. Signore Matteo was encouraged to recall his triumphs at the Fenice and, after a glass or two of del Collio, to describe his experiences during the Austrian siege of the city in '49. This was a tale which Mary had not heard.

". . . and when we had eaten," he told them, "I was brought to Daniele Manin. I have shaken him by the hand . . ."

He held out his quavering old hand as if it were a relic.

"And if you will believe me," boomed the Signora, "in those days he was slimmer than you, Sior Todaro; thin as Harlequin's wand he was in '49 . . . and I also!"

"And for what did we starve and suffer so?" demanded her

husband, his good humour suddenly vanished, "to have the accursed Whites strutting the streets again?"

Del Doria patted the old man on the shoulder and raised his glass.

"To that Day which will come!" he said.

They drank to that and the Signora rose.

"We will have music," she pronounced, "Maria will sing for us and, who knows, Enrico and I may even summon up the ghosts of our voices and sing as well..."

"Maria will sing 'Das Veilchen'," said her husband, " 'Das Veilchen' by Mozart that friend of freedom. Then we will see 'The Lover's Revenge' at the Marionette Theatre and forget our troubles."

This was not difficult. The Marionette Theatre was tiny and packed as full as it could hold of Venetians from every walk of life and of all ages; the audience enjoyed the play hugely and truth to be told it was extraordinarily appealing. The hero lamented the death of his heroine with passionate gestures of his jointed arms and legs and plotted the downfall of her murderer with a kind of ominous automatism. The villain's weathered wooden mask was a very nightmare of evil and when he died twitching and jerking upon the bed of ease procured for him by his villainy the audience was too impressed to cheer. The hero closed the piece by mourning the death of his humanity before he hanged himself. Mary was moved almost to tears by this mimic tragedy: de Doria's dark face mocked her sensibility in the candlelight, while all around, the Venetian cavaliers delighted in an excuse to distract their weeping companions.

"*Why* is it so...so moving?" she demanded in the interval, "At most operas I can only laugh at such fustian stuff; but this is different..."

Signor Matteo patted her hand.

"Because it is the reflection of our own situation," he explained, "we too are but poor creatures moved to and fro by circumstance. So... we feel for the poor puppets. Like us they have no reward but to be packed away in a box."

The next performance was by way of being an antidote to

such depressing thoughts upon the human condition. It concerned an Inn, run by one Harlequin and patronised by Pantaloon dressed in white military uniform with blue trousers, far too small for him and contending with a monstrous sword, which persecuted him at all points as he made a determined assault upon the virtue of the Columbine. In this nefarious enterprise he was assisted by a villainous doctor who provided him with a drug. Enter the deus et machina in the shape of a pig dressed in a travesty of a uniform, greeted by the audience with infinite delight, which drove the doctor and Pantaloon from the stage and left Columbine to the embraces of Harlequin. The curtain fell amid cries demanding to see again that 'angel of a pig' "! That they did not, could have been due to two unamused figures standing by the door who might or might not have been informers.

The following day Mary heard without surprise that Uncle Todaro had set the cat among the pigeons again by arriving at the dance only an hour before it ended.

"All the lemon-faces were furious and saying it was high time he settled down. And when he did come he didn't dance, just greeted the Contessa and went to smoke with the menfolk. The Mamas were fit to be tied!"

Mary smiled at this picture. She did not smile at the other piece of information.

"And as for Pietro . . . he behaved quite abominably," said his sister, "he didn't dance once, not once. He spent the whole night talking with some young men in the anteroom."

"Talking politics, I expect," said Mary, "you know what he is."

Giannina shook her head.

"Oh, no," she protested, "it was all perfectly friendly."

Mary laughed at this naive observation but after a moment's reflection seemed to hear the thorns crackling. A lack of argument pointed to a degree of agreement. She could bear to know what it was that Pietro and the young Carbonari were agreed about.

6

"Farewell, o, flowery haven!"

Madame Butterfly: PUCCINI

WITH THE COMING OF summer the atmosphere in the city changed. There was a tension in the air, a feeling of violence not far below the surface. Visitors were fewer than usual and those who came found the despairing poverty of many of the citizens distressing. The Austrians stationed there found it safer not to walk alone about the city and the number of Venetians in jail increased steadily. This, however, made no difference to the number of 'incidents'. The illegal news sheets sold better than the official journals and were read openly and defiantly in the cafés . . . there was, after all, a limit to the capacity of the jail. The Teatro Benedetto reopened to accommodate the visitors, but the officers from the garrison seldom went. Signor Carettoni found another diva who might be said to have attained the years of discretion . . . at all events she attracted no rival suitors to the theatre; though this might have had something to do with the fact that the illegal news sheets were now being distributed from another centre. The Austriacanti found the tide of feeling running strongly against them, and left to spend the summer in the High Adige 'for the sake of their health'. The heat increased and with it the tension.

On the surface life seemed very much what it had been since the city picked up the threads of living after the Austrian siege of 1849. The poor begged, foraged and occasionally even worked to keep alive; the shopkeepers and merchants bemoaned the decline of trade and engaged in cut-throat competition for what remained; Society or those who deemed themselves to belong thereto, engaged in the usual activities. The women paid calls and gossiped endlessly about each other. Lovers were taken and discarded, scandals sprang up and died; the young men paraded their pomaded hair and elegant waistcoats in the cafés round the Piazza, ogling the signorinas who passed with their chaperones and gossipping quite as much as the women, though their scandals were leavened (if that were the word) with politics. In the evening there were parties : musical parties, literary parties, card parties . . . but at each gathering the same people talked the same scandal. Occasionally the apparent monotony of these proceedings would be disrupted by a flaring of emotion either personal or political : but these were soon forgotten or appeared to be.

However, the summer meant different things to different people. To Tia Caterina, a housekeeper of the old-fashioned sort, it meant time to be spent in the still-room. To her an apothecary's shop was a last resort : her vast black-covered commonplace book contained remedies (which she brewed herself) for most complaints. To be in the city during the summer, when the herbs which were the basis of her remedies were ripening around the Monte Colon fields and gardens, was an exasperation to her. Baskets of greenstuff arrived by train from the estate and she picked these over, animadverting on the deterioration caused by train journeys. The market women were bribed to find her particular samples and the gardens of their acquaintance ransacked to find what she needed. Even Sior Paolo gained a momentary remission of her ill-opinion when he obtained for her from his mother a basketful of lovage. In view of this it was not surprising that she should keep a careful eye on the ancient lime-tree which grew beside the well in the central court of the palazzo. One day shortly after Mary's excursion with del Doria, when it was heavy and fragrant with flowers, and the whole canopy alive with bees, Tia Caterina decided that it was the exact moment to collect and dry the flowers to store against the making of sleep-inducing tisanes for the Parona. Mary, who was drawn into these preparations, could not feel that the Parona really stood in need of this specific. Her ability to sleep was quite startling : she rose late, enjoyed a long siesta in the heat of the day, frequently 'recruited her energies' on a day-bed before the evening's engagements and, if there were none, retired early, with a glass of limeflower tisane.

Marco was told to gather the flowers, and to this end was provided with a basket and a ladder. He was also given a barrage of instruction as to how the flowers should be picked. When he made an apprehensive observation about the numbers of bees in the boughs he was supposed to strip of their honey-source, Tia Caterina bared her teeth and brandished an onion and a blue bag.

"Behold!" she cried, "I am prepared!"

With such assurance he had to be content so he leaned the ladder against the trunk and began to climb.

"Meess Maria!" shrilled Tia Caterina. She had paid Mary the undoubted compliment of treating her with same disrespect as she treated the family themselves. With Sior Paolo she was monolithically formal.

"How may I assist?" asked Mary.

"Of your goodness bring me the trays to dry them on," ordered the housekeeper, "they will need to be cleaned and aired in the sun. Take you this key. You will find them in the store-room below the music-room window."

Like most Venetian houses the palazzo made up for the absence of cellars by a number of storerooms on the ground floor. Mary came over to take the outheld key just as Marco came tumbling down the ladder and said breathlessly.

"Permit me . . . I will fetch them . . ."

Tia Caterina turned a grim grey eye upon him so that he quailed. She pointed her bony finger up into the lime-tree.

"Ascend!" she said.

Marco ascended a few steps but looked down unhappily when Mary took the key. When she unlocked the door the reason for his unhappiness became apparent at once. At one point in his brief but eventful career the military pig had spent some time in this storeroom. The stench was unmistakable. Mary took the trays from their place against the wall and hastily relocked the door. She brought the woven straw utensils over to the well-kerb where two maids, both with an eye to Marco high above them in the bee-loud glade, were drawing up water in a wooden bucket. As she passed under the tree Marco hissed down at her.

"Meess! Meess!"

She paused and looked up.

"Keep the key!" he mouthed at her, "keep the key. Give it to the Signorino."

He sounded positively agonised. It would probably be a good idea to prevent either the housekeeper or Sior Paolo from discovering the state of the store. Mary put the key into the pocket of her skirt, which being more for the accommodation of lace-edged handkerchiefs and similar female impedimenta than for holding a five-inch hand-wrought iron key weighing nearly half a pound, was somewhat stretched. Fortunately Tia Caterina was so concerned with the state of the trays that she did not notice at once the non-return of the key. She exclaimed in horror over the dust of two years and the smell ... faugh! Country-bred Sylvana put her neat snub nose to the plaited straw and pronounced her verdict.

"Pigs!" she said.

Mary quailed inwardly, and exclaimed outwardly over the dust she had got upon her skirts, and left the argument which was beginning between the housekeeper and Sylvana as to the best way to be rid of this most clinging aroma.

The urgency in Marco's voice had told her two things, that whatever Pietro was about Marco was also involved (and that was a comforting thought for Marco was large and possessed of a degree of commonsense), and that there was probably more in the air than the smell of a small, misused pig. Pietro was not in his room, nor in the schoolroom, so she locked the unwieldy object in her desk and put the key to that on a ribbon round her neck.

It was eventually decided that the trays should be burned and new ones purchased. Mary offered to go out and try to find some. Marco, who by this time had picked three basketsful of the sweet limeblossom and collected as many beestings, was grateful to be excused further duty on the ladder in order to be her escort. As they walked to the narrow alleyway where the basket-makers had their booths, he explained that he and Pietro had taken the key from Guiseppe's drawer when the pig arrived from Monte Colon.

"For it is never used . . . never in my knowledge. We had the pig there three days, Meess . . . and I had to feed him five times a day so that he would not squeal, and the Signorino bought laudanum to quiet him so that we could put the clothes upon him . . ."

He chuckled showing his beautiful white teeth.

"Mother of God, what a task was that!" he exclaimed, "May I never have to do the same again . . ."

Mary had a sudden mental image of the quiet body of the young Austrian soldier floating face-downward . . .

"But we didn't know that the Old Dragon had a key as well," he went on, "it was a bad moment that . . . phew!"

"Where is the Signorino today?" Mary interrupted him.

Marco shrugged.

"He has some meetings, I expect. Those . . . they are like children, his new friends. Always these meetings and passwords and such toys. And now there is to be another . . ."

He pulled himself up suddenly, looking sidelong at Mary.

"But me . . . I know nothing."

"Not another unfortunate pig, I hope," said Mary lightly.

Marco shook his head.

On their return with the new trays they found there was a fine hue and cry for the key, that the store might be opened and cleansed. Mary her face solemn and worried declared that she had brought the key back with her . . . which was true as far as it went.

"You might not recall," she suggested to the housekeeper, "you were so much occupied. Did you perhaps place it upon the kerb of the well when you examined the trays?"

Tia Caterina threw up her hands in horror at the idea, and set such members of the household as could be spared from the preparation of dinner to examine the courtyard inch by inch: but, not surprisingly, to no avail. Guiseppe, woken from a prolonged siesta, reminded them smugly that Tia Caterina had taken all the store keys in hand as soon as she arrived, and then retired to his room. Sior Paolo considered the scene and sniffed thoughtfully at the locked door but offered no comment. The key was finally given up for lost in the depths of the Murano well and it was decided to send for the locksmith in the morning : at this Mary felt tolerably secure for no Venetian tradesman ever arrived upon the first summons.

Pietro did not return for dinner and the household had retired to bed, before Mary heard a sound in the corridor outside her room, just as she was brushing out her hair. She rose and slipped on her wrapper before opening her door. The corridor was empty and dark but there was a glimmer of light — candle-light — under the schoolroom door. As silently as she could she crossed the passage and lifted the latch. The door moved open and she peeped round it intending to give Pietro a well-deserved start. She opened her mouth to demand what he was thinking of to be out till midnight and then closed it again. The portly figure presently engaged in trying to pick the lock of her desk was not Pietro, it was Sior Paolo. She dodged back out of sight thinking very quickly; the steward might pick the lock with her goodwill for he would find nothing but writing paper, ink and pens. The key for which he was almost certainly searching was now safely under her pillow. From a number of small signs which she had scarcely noticed before, displaced ornaments, mispaired shoes and disarranged drawers, she realised that her own room had been thoroughly searched while she was out. She hoped that Pietro had left nothing incriminating in his room but could place no dependence upon it.

She withdrew from the door as silently as she had come and closed it, holding her breath. She tiptoed back to her own room and closed the door confident that Sior Paolo had not seen her. In this she was wrong. The draught from the open door had made his candle flare and waver and as soon as the door was shut again he had extinguished it, and opened the door a crack to see who it was had seen him. The dim light of Mary's bedside candle had been enough to show him her tall figure and long golden hair.

While Mary made plans to write to del Doria in the morning and tell him that it looked rather as if Sior Paolo had decided to go fishing for sprats, Sior Paolo padded back to his room and laid a few plans of his own.

The evening following these events Signora Murano planned to give a musical soirée, and a question had arisen as to the best method of decorating the small salon which was also the music room. This apartment had a somewhat enervating, sub-aqueous air, which was produced by faded blue-green hangings, a green and white marble terrazzo floor and a set of murals of the eighteenth century depicting Neptune among Nereids, whose attributes were enhanced rather than concealed by the artist's tactful use of sea-foam. Modern tastes rejected the subject of one panel, where naked and shameless boys rode dolphins through improbable waves, and curtains had been hung before it. This circumstance, Mary noticed, served to stimulate interest in art among the Signora's visitors who, if ushered into this room to wait upon their hostess, immediately peeped behind the curtain to dicover what chef d'oeuvre might thus be protected from the light of common day.

It had been decided that a quantity of white and yellow flowers would alleviate this submarine quality, and it was for these that Mary was to visit the Rialto market in the very early morning. Tia Caterina had professed herself too busy to go with her and Giannina, more honestly, declined to rise at five in the morning. Mary's companion was thus to be Sior Paolo who discovered an errand to the wine merchants. They met upon the steps of the Palazzo in the fresh morning air and smiled falsely upon one another. Mary made some remark about its being the best part of the day to which the steward assented very politely and improved the occasion with a well-worn remark about spending the best part of the day in bed. This exchange of conversational small change was terminated by the arrival of a yawning and apologetic Alessandro.

When Alessandro landed them at the Pontile Cerva they agreed to meet again in an hour, so that he could take them back with their purchases. Mary made her way over the ancient bridge with her customary pleasure in its elegance and found herself in the noisy confusion of the market. Sior Paolo watched her out of sight. As far as Mary could discover, the only people who were not clamouring at the very pitch of their lungs were herself, and the Gobbo who frowned thoughtfully at the stones below him as he had done for centuries. The flower-boats lay beyond the Fabbriche Vecchio and she picked her way there slowly between the pyramids of cabbages and the carefully arranged piles of melons and cucumbers. Wreaths of golden onions and snowy-white garlic decorated the stalls, and everywhere there was the smell of fried eels, polenta and the powerful Venetian soup called squassetto, on which the market people were breakfasting between an argument and a bargain. Mary sniffed appreciatively; her breakfast had been a cup of buttermilk and the memory of hungry days at the Calle di Fuseri was still fresh. She did not notice the sour looks or hear the obscene comments which were called forth by her height and colouring; nor did she see Sior Paolo, his errand to the wine merchant either finished or forgotten, go to the fried-eel stall at which he dispensed hospitality to certain hungry persons and contrived to insert some mistaken notions in their heads at the same time as he put polenta and fried eel in their bellies.

At the flower-stalls Mary's lavish requirements soon met an enthusiastic response, and her evident and unteutonic delight in a bargain dispelled suspicion. She chaffered over a few soldi as if they had been her own, and the posy-sellers, hovering like seagulls for broken and discarded blooms which they could make up into their plate-like posies, recognised a noble encounter and gathered round screaming encouragement to both sides. Such a scene might have dispelled the inaccurate notions inspired by Sior Paolo among the lasagnoni now approaching the group, but for one unfortunate circumstance. An English visitor, Baedeker in hand, and advised by his courier to see his chosen sights in the early morning, was making enquiries at the edge of the group as to the whereabouts of the Ca'd'oro. He was of the school which believes that all foreigners can understand plain English if it is spoken loudly enough, so Mary heard him even above the market-women. Breaking off an impassioned denunciation of the price of the yellow roses she had decided to buy, she directed him, in English. This was enough to convince Sior Paolo's dupes — here was an Austrian, speaking shamelessly in what must be the hated tongue of the oppressor; what was more she was a mere female (albeit large) and unaccompanied . . .

'A abbasso Austriaci !' the chant began and was taken up enthusiastically by other hangers-on . . . white uniforms were not in evidence at that hour. The crowd grew in size and hostility.

Mary did not at once realise that the cry was directed at herself; but when the woman she was bargaining with looked apprehensively over Mary's shoulder into the crowd and then jumped down into her boat to push it away from the quay, the position became plain. It also became plain that she was in some danger. Girls brought up as she had been, had little opportunity to learn to swim, and standing as she did on the edge of the quay, it looked as if she would have to remedy this rather suddenly. Abruptly she sat down on a fruit-barrow. She was not going to be forced into the Canalazzo simply by the pressure of the crowd about her. If she was going in, the crowd would have to pick her up and throw her in. She was conscious not of fear but of anger at such a ridiculous misunderstanding. Her protests were drowned by the shouting and those who might have protested more forcibly had been pushed or frightened away. The English visitor by now some distance away, heard the commotion but did not remark on its difference from the racket of foreign sounds which had assailed his ears since he had reached the Rialto.

Mary heard the filthy abuse aimed at her and felt the barrow shift as dirty hands grabbed at it and rocked it hoping to dislodge her into the canal; her anger gave way at last to fear. Unless one of the nearby fruitboats defied the crowd and came to her assistance she would certainly drown. It was exasperating to be drowned for an ignorant mistake and for one's death to be a Piazza joke, as hers undoubtedly would be, was the ultimate humiliation. The barrow rose in the air and Mary clung to the sides with a cataleptic grip. A cruel blow on her fingers failed to break it and before the blow could be repeated, a yell of fury was heard, as the owner of the barrow clawed his way through in a fruitless attempt to rescue his melons and apricots now floating disconsolately on the green water. He was a little disconcerted to find Mary on the barrow in their place and the object of this hostility, but it did not prevent his laying about him with a boat-hook which forced the crowd back. Mary looked about her for another weapon but there was none to be had. All round the Campo shutters were opening and heads emerged to view the fracas.

The crowd closed in again and Mary realised that the barrow-owner's intervention had been a reprieve and not a rescue. She was conscious of a hope that he could swim and wished, as on other, less fraught occasions, that her cavalier was a foot taller and a stone or two heavier. If he had to pull her waterlogged frame to shore ... a picture of a steamer being hauled into port by a minute tug came into her mind's eye and she laughed. Her cavalier began to lay about him with the boat-hook, while Mary frustrated those who wished to disarm him, by driving the barrow hard against their shins, a course approved by the owner of the barrow in wild battle cries. The absurdity of the situation suddenly overcame Mary and again she had to laugh aloud as she lamed another onslaught of lasagnoni. Her defender evidently approved of her tactics for he yelled.

"Brava, la Gigantessa! Brava!"

and laid open the head of the largest of Sior Paolo's breakfast guests with a shrewd blow of his boat-hook. The mob hesitated at this unexpected casualty and hovered undecidedly, yelling abuse; just at that point rescue arrived from all sides at once to end the desperate battle of the barrow.

From the fruitmarket there came running a tall, familiar figure, his face distorted with anger, brandishing a black cane and shouting furious orders. He had been roused from an early breakfast in his lodging on the Campo Battisti by a gleeful report from his manservant, that an Austrian whore was going to be ducked in the canal, and had deduced from his description who she might be. From the other side came Alessandro with half a dozen well-muscled gondoliers brandishing oars, and Angelo with a yelling horde of bold, bad street-urchins at his back all armed with rotting fruit discarded from the boats. This they hurled with a precision and force gained in their campaigns against the innumerable cats of Venice.

The mob assailed on three sides broke up and ran. Alessandro and his friends heaved some of them into the canal and watched their splashings and blowings with satisfaction. Angelo, making painful use of his elbows, dived through to Mary's side and demanded to learn at once what injury had been done her and by whom, so that he might fry the culprit's liver in his own lard and eat it in the Piazza. Mary insisted that she was quite intact; not so much as a scratch. She had only lost her hat, a nice blond straw, for which she had had an affection, and which now bobbed among the melons, apricots and assorted, spluttering lasagnoni. This was enough for Angelo who ordered one of his army into the water with the air of a Toussaint l'Ouverture. Thus it was that when del Doria had dispersed the remnant of Mary's attackers with hard blows and even harder words, he found Mary sitting on the barrow trying to dry with an inadequate pocket-handkerchief a naked, proud and dripping urchin, whose only adornment was a sodden straw hat. Meanwhile Angelo danced in triumph on the quay, and frustrated the efforts of some aquatic anti-Austrians to haul themselves up out of the water. This he did by jumping on their fingers with his wooden shoes, an exercise which Mary, whose own fingers were swollen and painful, felt was no more than they deserved. In the intervals of wringing out the handkerchief she was trying to thank the owner of the barrow for his knight-errantry while he assured her, though without the ring of true conviction, what the loss of his whole day's stock-in-trade was a small price to pay for the privilege of defending a woman of such spirit and bravery . . . surely the daughter of many brave soldiers!

"You're not hurt?" del Doria asked of Mary and she shook her head.

"But this poor man . . ." she explained, "he has lost all his fruit on my behalf because I chose to sit upon his barrow. I would be infinitely obliged, Signor, if you would lend me enough to buy him replacements . . ."

She gave the rescuer of her hat a light spank on his bare backside as an indication that he could resume his breeches.

". . . and perhaps a few coins to buy this poor little one a bowl of squassetto to drive out the wet. You see I have no money with me which is my own."

"It will be a pleasure, Signorina."

He smiled and took his opportunity to distribute largesse on a scale which Mary could never have repaid, not only to Angelo's lieutenant and the owner of the barrow but also to Angelo and Alessandro. He turned back from this pleasing occupation to find the ex-maiden-in-distress calmly concluding her business with the proprietrix of the roses. She was indicating Alessandro, now assisting the exit of a wet lasagnono by a kick in his breeches.

"Below the Rialto in fifteen minutes."

"Understood, Signorina. They will be there."

Del Doria considered her with a marked degree of amusement.

"Tell me, Signorina, is there nothing which could happen to overset your composure?"

She coloured slightly at this but did not, he noted with approval, ask him what he meant.

"I suppose I could be said to have developed an immunity to drama," she remarked and turned her attention to a purveyor of sun-flowers, "I suspect it comes of a surfeit of opera."

"Indeed?"

"My mother, my father, my stepmother and my sister," she explained, "they were all singers with the opera . . ."

She picked out a dozen vast and glowing blooms.

". . . and either you become resistant to opera, I find, or you become soaked in it. In our house, Signor, a burned toast resulted in the Mad Scene from *Lucia di Lammermoor*."

Del Doria laughed at this picture and took the top-heavy bundle from her while she paid.

"I reacted against this, I suppose. After a time not only did the burned toast not seem worth the commotion but I came to the conclusion that there was really very little which was. It used to irritate my sister beyond words..."

Del Doria stopped in his tracks and began to laugh.

"That I can imagine!"

"And then of course," Mary went on, "the Italians expect the English to 'have phlegm'. Do you not find that you become what people expect?"

Del Doria agreed enthusiastically.

"But of course," he said, "it saves one so much exertion."

Mary smiled.

"What do people expect of you?" she enquired.

"Very little," he admitted. "I should be elegantly idle, ornament society and provide a little gossip. I should philander a little where it will do no harm..."

He raised his eyebrows.

"...and of course I must run like a rabbit from the matchmaking mamas. I find all this comes easily to one of my temperament."

"To be idle, elegantly or otherwise, hardly consorts with being abroad before seven," observed Mary.

"But you are quite out," demurred her escort, "I had not yet retired..."

It was Mary's turn to laugh.

They came to the Rialto and began to climb the steps.

"You puzzle me," he said suddenly, "your beautiful Italian... How long have you been in Italy?"

"I was born here," she said. "We went to England only once until my father died."

"Have you relatives in England?"

She shrugged.

"Aunt Amelia... my father's sister. She is the only woman who can look me in the eye. And a cousin or so. After my father died we went home to stay with her for a time. I found a post with a school and was happy enough, but Flora could not bear the wet and the cold..."

She pulled herself up.

"But you must have heard all this from Flora."

"Oh, no," he said, "conversation with your sister rarely touched on such mundane topics as aunts and cousins . . ."

Mary raised her eyebrows. While she owned to a family affection for her erratic sister, she had to admit that even her most devoted admirer could never describe Flora as a notable conversationalist. Either del Doria had tapped unsuspected deeps or he was . . .

"At the risk of offending your sisterly loyalties," he went on, "I have to confess that my own discourse had to be couched in terms of extravagant flattery to be at all acceptable while her own took the form of complaint . . . your sister, Miss Maria, could complain at greater length about matters of the smallest moment than any other woman of my acquaintance. And I have a wide female acquaintance most of whom concern themselves constantly with matters of small moment."

Mary paused at the top of the arch. She found herself unable to comment : it was not that she found del Doria's description of Flora's conversation inaccurate or unjust, she too had suffered from Flora's lengthy analyses of imaginary slights from her fellow-players, it was that del Doria's irony raised a question in her mind, a question quite impossible to ask. He looked at her quizzically and she had an odd sensation that he guessed at her thoughts. Fleetingly she wondered why he should say such a thing to her : it was when she came to think about it, a breach of good manners, something which she, for one, would *not* expect of him. His motive in this was obscure, or perhaps it would be truer to say that his only possible motive was not credible . . . to Mary at all events.

They descended the far side of the Rialto in silence. Alessandro was waiting, his boat filled with roses but there was no sign of Paolo. Del Doria handed her in and stepped down after her.

"I think we won't wait for the steward, Alessandro," he said. "The Palazzo Murano."

"Understood," said Alessandro with emphasis. He had a tale to tell the Signor which he had learned from one of the lasagnoni. He thought it unlikely that Sior Paolo would keep his rendezvous.

"But," Mary protested, "I did say ..."

Del Doria looked at his companion closely as Alessandro made his way through the press of boats.

"I want to get you home as soon as possible. Despite that calm exterior I suspect you are more shaken than you care to admit."

"Well, of course I don't care to admit it," returned Mary acidly, "not my style at all. Can you see me fainting from shock? It might be the Campanile collapsing. It is a little difficult to play the fragile and delicate female when you must first look round for four strong men."

Del Doria chuckled once more at this riposte.

"And why was it that you alone escaped an operatic fate?" he asked after a short silence.

"If I had been contralto," admitted Mary, "it might not have been so easy, but I had the good sense to be a soprano ..."

She smiled happily.

"Most tenors draw the line at singing deathless devotion to someone's stomach," she explained, "and one can't always be reclining on a sofa ... it takes up too much room ..."

She hesitated.

"Besides ... perhaps it is just sour grapes with me ... but I really had no wish to sing operatic roles. They are many of them so *silly*. Am I treading on your toes? Are you an opera-lover?"

"No," admitted del Doria, "with a few notable exceptions I find most operas extremely tedious. My opera-going is usually done with ulterior motives ..."

He gave a sly side-glance at Mary who raised her eyebrows.

"Understood," she told him drily.

"... usually political," he continued as if she had not spoken, "as many of my actions are. I ask you to believe this."

His face was unsmiling and Mary found herself disconcerted.

The gondola grated alongside and he jumped out to help her ashore.

"Should Alessandro take the flowers round to the other landing?" he asked.

Mary agreed to this and laid the sunflowers on the sweet-smelling pile of roses in the forepart, then reached up her hand to him. He took it but did not grasp it.

"Did they do *this* to you, those bastards?" he asked, his voice vicious and Alessandro exclaimed in reproof.

Mary drew her hand away and reached up the other one. The short journey had permitted the bruises on her fingers to swell and discolour and she had had no chance to wipe away the blood from the grazes ...

"It is nothing of any consequence," she told him.

"You will permit me to be the judge of that," he said, "and if I find the mongrel dog who did it I ..."

"I beg you will not inform Angelo," Mary interrupted, her eyes twinkling, "or he will fry his liver in the Piazza, he told me so."

"And I will bring the salt ..." promised Alessandro.

"Let it not escape your attention," Mary pointed out, "that the episode arose from a misunderstanding. The poor, dear, patriotic fellows mistook me for an Austrian whore ... or so I understood them ..."

That evening del Doria raised the Mamas' expectations by appearing at his sister's soirée and listening with every symptom of attention to a number of offerings (sacrifices might have been a more appropriate word in some cases), upon the altar of St Cecilia. He shocked them halfway through the evening by leaving his place among a selection of eligible damsels and having a conversation with 'that beanpole of a governess ... the one with the sister ... you remember ...' Mary had spent the evening accompanying the singers and instrumentalists. They would have been more shocked had they heard the conversation.

"You spend your time cultivating sand, Signorina, and washing Ethiopians."

"Oh, come," said Mary, "they are not as bad as all that."

"They are not," he agreed, "they are worse, much worse. How is your hand? This is no way to heal it."

She tucked it under a fold of her scarf.

"Better," she told him.

"Brazen liar," he told her and grinned.

"Are you going to sing tonight?"

She shook her head.

"My hand is much too sore for that, Signor."

He plucked that maltreated member out of hiding and kissed it lightly.

"In that case," he announced, "I have nothing to wait for. Tell me, where is your other charge tonight?"

"Pietro? Oh, such an evening was not for him. He blanched at the very thought."

Del Doria raised his eyebrows.

"He will sing another tune when he develops an interest over there."

He nodded at the cluster of conscious girls preparing to delight their hearer again.

"Possibly," agreed Mary. "However, at the moment his interests are those of his uncle. Political."

He gave a delighted laugh and flung up his hand in a gesture she recognised as a fencer's.

"Colpo! Colpo!" he admitted.

With that he left, dashing the Mamas' expectations and exposing Mary to some exquisite insolence, which should have scarified her if she had had any attention to spare for it. Her time was fully occupied in telling herself fiercely that his motives for kissing her hand were completely political. Giannina came over wide-eyed.

"Zia Margarita is trying to make Mama turn you off," she confided.

"Dear me," remarked Mary, "is she succeeding? Should I go to pack my trunk?"

"Not yet," advised Giannina, "Mama just says yes and amen and looks sleepy."

"How distressing for your Aunt, the Contessa," said Mary primly and reprovingly, "you should have more sympathy."

Giannina giggled.

Sior Paolo did not return that day, or any other. Guiseppe

with an intolerable air of "I-told-you-so' resumed his duties, or some of them.

A week after the soirée it became very hot. Mary found it hard to sleep one night and deciding that it was not sensible to lie awake wishing for sleep, had lit a candle and was reading *Northanger Abbey*. She found Miss Austen a reliable antidote to Italy, heat and melodrama. The General had just evicted poor Catherine when she was startled back into Italy by an explosion which shook the whole Palazzo. She dropped the book and ran to the window which looked along the Salizzeria San Pantalon. A pall of smoke billowed up, blotting out the stars and was lit from below by a flickering red and yellow glare : from what she could make out, it arose from the railway station or from somewhere near there. There was a barracks, she recalled, next to Little San Simeon across the Ponte degli Scalzi : that was probably the target for the . . . her hands suddenly prickled and she felt an icy wrench in her stomach. Del Doria's voice saying, 'I have a notion they have got their hands on something more dangerous than a pig', was so clear that he might have been in the room. She seized her dressing-gown and raced barefoot along the passage pulling it over her nightgown. The room to which Pietro had retired soon after dinner, 'to do some work on Signor Peeckweeck before Meess Maria pulls my ears for idleness . . .' was empty. The light of the fire in the sky was enough to show his bed empty and unruffled, his nightshirt and cap still undisturbed upon the coverlet. The schoolroom next door was empty too.

Back in her own room Mary scrambled herself into some clothes, and then went downstairs to try to find a messenger she could send to the Campo Battisti : she found a light in the hall and Marco noisily asleep in the porter's chair. She shook him awake.

"Signorina !"

"Hush ! What are you doing up at this time of the night?"

Marco rubbed his eyes and tried to collect his wits.

"I must have . . ." he began.

"No lies!" said Mary fiercely, "Is it the Signorino?"

He nodded his round face serious for once.

"Were you to let him in?"

"Yes. He did not wish to leave the house unlocked in these times."

"I'm glad he'd that much sense."

Mary pulled back the bolts of the door which gave on to the Salizzeria and Marco got to his feet and helped her.

"What's afoot?" he asked anxiously.

"You must sleep like Barbarossa, Marco," said Mary setting the door about a foot ajar, "There was an explosion and a fire."

She pointed at the angry red of the sky to the west.

"Signorino Pietro's room is empty . . . and I find you here. It seems fairly obvious what's afoot."

Marco scratched his tousled head and said nothing, his eyes on the Salizzeria. Suddenly he stiffened and pointed. The lamp under the shrine on the corner gave very little light but it was enough to show a movement as someone came past. There was also a sound of running footsteps and someone sobbing for breath.

Pietro covered the last few yards to the door and practically fell inside. Even in the dim light of Marco's flickering lamp they could see his face was ashen-white and his mouth set in a line which told of pain. He held his right elbow cupped in his left hand and there was something wrong about the outline of his shoulder.

"Shut door!" he gasped and Marco obeyed, thrusting the bolts home. Mary touched his sleeve.

"You're soaked to the bone!" she exclaimed.

"Fell . . ." muttered Pietro, ". . . canal . . ."

He gave a little sigh and crumpled up against her.

7

"She has flown, The Turtle-Dove . . ."

Tales of Hoffman: OFFENBACH

PIETRO WAS DISCOVERED TO have a dislocated shoulder. Marco looked up from this discovery.

"I can put it right," he assured Mary, "I know how, my father showed me. Best to do it while he feels nothing. Hold him so."

He arranged the limp figure across Mary's knee and gave a sickening jerk and twist to the distorted joint. Mary heard a muffled sound as the humerus returned to its socket and hoped she would not complicate the situation by being sick.

"I'll fetch the brandy," offered Marco.

"No," she said. "I imagine there will be soldiers here at any minute. Go to Signor del Doria in the Campo Battisti; tell him what has happened. Stay there. If you come back they will want to know where you have been. Tomorrow, if I can, I'll come to the market. You can bring me any message there. Now hurry! Take boat . . . there should be some at the San Polo Bridge."

Marco did not argue. He drew back the bolts, opened the door and vanished into the darkness like a hunted cat. Mary replacing the bolts, thought she could just hear the clatter of booted feet coming along the Salizzeria at speed. She returned hurriedly to Pietro who was beginning to revive. He groaned and opened his eyes.

"My arm," he muttered, "it hurts . . ."

"Bound to," said Mary, "but I expect you'll be able to use it a little now. Can you stand up? I must get you upstairs if I can."

He allowed her to pull him up and stood swaying. She put his sound arm across her shoulder and they moved up the stair-case.

"The petard went off too soon," he explained, "before we were clear. Beam or something fell on me. I went in the canal. Bruno hauled me out but they saw us and chased . . . Bruno tried to take them off towards the Guidecca but they split up . . . they're after me now."

"I know," she said. "In here . . ."

She steered him into the schoolroom passage and along to his own room at the end of it. She was just lowering him into the chair when they heard shouts and a hammering on the door which gave on to the Salizzeria.

"Let's hope that Guiseppe can delay them for a while. He can be very slow when he wants to. If we can just get you into bed and be rid of those wet clothes we can protest that you have never been out of the house."

But this was not so easy: the buttonholes of his coat and waistcoat had shrunk and so had the material. The wet lining of his coat caught and dragged painfully on his swollen shoulder. Down in the hall Guiseppe, already awakened by the explosion had appeared with unaccustomed speed, his thin white hair in an astonished halo round his head. The Wachtmeister in charge of the squad which clattered into the hall brushed aside the old man's protests and made for the staircase. Clearly they were familiar with the geography of the house. Sior Paolo had not wasted the time since his disappearance.

"Young ruffian better not try to run for it," the Wachtmeister told Guiseppe harshly. "I've stopped the boltholes . . . he'll get a bullet in his belly if he tries it."

He snapped an order at four of the panting detachment and they clattered upstairs and along the uncarpeted corridor. At Pietro's door the Wachtmeister raised the latch and kicked open the door.

Pietro was alone, facing the door, in his shirt and trousers, his face as white as his shirt. When they had heard the soldiers in the passage he had thrust Mary through the connecting door into the schoolroom.

"You're not to get tangled up in this . . ." he told her urgently, "tell Papa or someone. They know it was me. I was seen. I'll have to go with them."

Mary did not wait to argue. From the schoolroom it was possible to go through Giannina's room to her own. Giannina was awake and frightened. Mary whispered to her to lie low and vanished into her own room where she pulled on her dressing-gown over her clothes. Candle in hand, she emerged into the corridor just as Pietro was being marched off in the centre of four soldiers, the Wachtmeister in front, and Guiseppe hovering unhappily behind. The Wachtmeister blanched slightly at the apparition in front of him which was indeed sufficiently alarming. Mary, all in white, her hair wildly untidy and her face pale, with a candle casting her huge distorted shadow over the end of the passage, looked more like an avenging ghost than she realised. One of the soldiers who might have had reason to fear such an apparition, hoarsely besought the Virgin to protect him and crossed himself.

"And what is this?" asked the apparition angrily. "What do you mean by disturbing a respectable household in the middle of the night?"

"This young ruffian'll tell you that," said the Wachtmeister, reassured by this prosaic demand that she was no spectral visitation. He could deal with mere mortal females.

"Stand aside," he told her roughly.

Mary did not move.

"Are you arresting him?"

"We are," said the Wachtmeister.

"Without informing even his parents?"

"You'll do that soon enough."

"Well," said Mary, "I had heard that the Tedeschi were brutal and high-handed but I would never have believed that they waged war on children!"

The Wachtmeister flushed at this contemptuous nickname and thrust his musket at her.

"Stand out of the way!"

She ignored him and raised the candle to look at Pietro.

"But he is soaking wet!"

138

Pietro found himself able to smile at the note of surprise.

"And not allowed to take so much as a shirt with him! The thoughtlessness, the arrogance ... it could happen only here. Guiseppe, of your goodness pack a bag for the Signorino," she told the trembling old man who went at once.

The Wachtmeister pushed his gun into Mary's face and glowered.

"It's me giving the orders here," he told her. "I won't wait for no bag. Stand aside!"

"But his clothes are wet! He will catch his death ..."

Such a protest provoked an expression of sardonic amusement on the soldier's face, which sent a chill down her spine. Reluctantly she stood aside.

"Where shall we send his clothes?" she demanded.

"To the New Prisons," he flung over his shoulder and added gloatingly, "but you'd better make haste if the young shaver's to make any use of them."

The delay had been long enough to permit the rest of the household to make its appearance: the servants milled noisily in the hall and Signor and Signora Murano stood whitefaced but calm on the landing as their son was marched out of the house. He gave them one unhappy glance, smiled unconvincingly and was gone.

Guiseppe with a hastily packed cloak-bag pattered in pursuit. Mary stood at the head of the staircase thinking what else she could do and Giannina crept out of her room and came to stand beside her. The heavy door slammed behind the detachment with a doleful final sound. Signora Murano who had seemed to be in a kind of trance began to cry hysterically. Mary moved towards her but was forestalled by the Paron who put his arms round his wife and looked at Mary over her heaving shoulders, his face grey and set.

"That petard? The explosion," he asked, "was he involved in that?"

Mary nodded.

"Marco has taken word to the Campo Battisti," she told him very quietly.

"Good."

He looked momentarily relieved.

"God send Todaro is in his own bed," he added.

Tia Caterina came clucking up the staircase with her hair in a marvellous array of curl-papers. She enveloped her Parona in sympathy, persuading her to return to bed: the Parona went with her like a child. Her husband looked bereft.

"Todaro *warned* me," he said and struck his hand on the banister-rail, "he warned me but I was rude. I told him to mind his own business and let me mind mine. I was sure he was too young to be up to anything so dangerous ... so foolhardy. I should have known. He is the image of my father ... and I should have known, if anyone did ..."

Mary said nothing.

"I suppose he warned you too?"

She nodded. Her employer's mouth twisted as if he had tasted something unpleasant.

"A man of discernment, my brother-in-law, for all his frivolity."

He raised his voice.

"Back to bed, all of you!" he ordered harshly, "there is nothing more we can do. And my hands are tied ... tied fast."

The household gradually obeyed but they were no sooner settled down to wait for morning, when they were roused again by musket-butts applied to the door without finesse. The Wachtmeister had returned and this time he was not triumphant, he was in a tearing rage. The whole household was turned out and herded into the hall. The Palazzo was searched from top to bottom. The soldiers ran bayonets through sacks and mattresses, turned the contents of chests and trunks out on to the floor, and with ready fingers on their triggers discouraged protests at the damage they did. A supercilious officer presided over this orgy, standing in the hall, arms folded receiving a series of negative reports from the sweating soldiery. When it was abundantly plain that whatever the Austrians were searching for was not to be found, this officer beckoned to Signor Murano who was sitting at the foot of the staircase.

The Paron looked at the white-uniformed intruder with a stony lack of response and stood his ground; after a somewhat tense moment the officer strode over to him.

"Where is he?" he demanded abruptly.

The Paron said nothing but Giannina crouched on the staircase with a Paisley shawl tucked about her raised her head at such a question.

"Where is who?" she asked, puzzled.

"Do you think you can play your lying games with me," the officer snarled and struck the Paron on the breastbone with the hilt of his sword so hard that he gasped for breath.

"Where have you got him hidden?" he shouted. "We'll find him you know . . . wherever you've got him stowed away!"

"He means Pietro," said Mary under her breath and a great weight seemed to lift off her, "he means Pietro . . . he's escaped, he must have!"

Beside her Giannina jumped and squeaked slightly with excitement at this conclusion. The officer looked murderously at the Paron and lifted his sword again . . . this time the blade was foremost and he had his eyes on Giannina.

"We were under the impression that *you* had him," said Mary in a clear carrying voice and rose to her feet, "surely you haven't succeeded in mislaying him already?"

There was a provocative ring of contemptuous amusement in her voice. The officer lost interest in the Paron and advanced upon Mary who looked down at him in her customary unruffled fashion.

"And you know nothing of this . . . oh, no, nothing!"

His voice was viciously sarcastic.

"No," said Mary.

"Then how did you know he had escaped?"

Mary laughed.

"I drew that conclusion from your speedy return, your evident ill-temper and your bad manners . . . not to mention the damage you permitted your ham-handed yokels to do . . ."

There was a small sound of indrawn breath as Mary read in her opponent's narrowed eyes a strong desire to do her some grievous injury, but she had judged her man correctly and her diversion succeeded. He thrust the sword back in its scabbard and shouted an order at the Wachtmeister.

"I am leaving a guard here," he flung at the Paron, "they will catch your pup when he comes crawling home. Feed them or it'll be the worse for you!"

With that he withdrew leaving the Wachtmeister and a half-dozen soldiers.

For the second time that night the Murano household dispersed, this time to remedy the unbelievable disorder created by the search. Mary folded clothes and repacked chests and drawers thinking hard all the while. It would seem that del Doria had moved very swiftly indeed. There had been a rescue before Pietro could vanish into the deeps of the New Prisons. The next problem would no doubt be to get him out of Venice. That charming city was a little like a trap. She wondered briefly about Bruno and the rest of the Young Carbonari; but her mind revolved mostly about the explosion. What had the young brutes blown up, and how many poor souls had they killed or injured?

Morning brought rumours and then news. The barracks near the station had had the façade blown right out; seven Austrian soldiers were dead, many were injured. Mary heard this with a sinking heart; no schoolboy prank this, it was a hanging or a shooting matter. Signor Murano's face did not betray his feelings at the news but when he left the table, Mary thought inconsequently that he was smaller than she had thought.

The household found themselves under close surveillance. Mary demanding to visit the market to buy food to fill all those extra mouths, found that she was to take a soldier with her for an escort. 'At least,' she reflected, 'there is no danger of being pushed into the Canalazzo today.' In fact murmurs of sympathy followed her round the stalls as the story of the previous night's events spread (with advantages). At last she caught sight of Marco. He was standing beside a posy-seller and looked straight at her without a sign of recognition. As Mary watched covertly she saw money change hands and the dark hook-nosed woman give her a searching look. It was now obvious where the communication would be, her aim must be to distract her escort's attention. This was not so difficult; during their progress through the market, there had been enough hard looks and imprecations flung at him to have shrivelled a sensitive man. Sensitivity, however, was not his outstanding characteristic. Mary saw him trying in vain to attract a kind glance from three handsome young fish-sellers posed by a fish-boat with their baskets on their heads. Mary, however, was not accustomed to carry her loads in such a convenient fashion and she had been refused the service of a man-servant to carry her basket. By this time it was heavily charged. With a sweet smile and a word of thanks she handed it to the soldier who was too taken aback to do other than accept it. This did at least gain him the attention of the three graces by the fish boat, who burst into unkind laughter at the figure he cut. It also amused a tall, unkempt figure who was watching the scene from beneath the brim of a disreputable straw hat underneath the Gobbo. Mary then appeared to notice a sweetmeat stall and moved swiftly towards it, her attendant trailing behind both hands on the handle of the basket, and his musket, the sling of which had slipped from his shoulder to the crook of his arm, getting awkwardly between his blue-clad legs. Behind him ran a comet-tail of jeering children. Mary bought some large almond comfits of a variety she knew to be both adhesive and long-lasting. With another smile she thrust the largest and stickiest between the soldier's parted lips as he shouted abuse at his tormentors; this action so embarrassed him he was forced to put down the basket and deal with the confection thus failing to notice her next transaction which was the purchase of one of those paper-framed posies from a dark hook-nosed woman.

With a glance at her thickly uniformed companion, now perspiring freely under the July sun, Mary gauged her next few purchases carefully: weight was a premier consideration. She added as an afterthought a trio of superb and enormous cabbages which weighed not a gramme less than eight kilos and two vast melons which balanced on the loaded basket only with difficulty and kept rolling off. Mary then decided to walk home rather than take boat and her escort had a certain amount of difficulty in matching her long stride.

Once back in the Palazzo the soldier, now as close to mutiny as he was ever likely to get, was directed to leave his load in the kitchen. Mary wondered briefly what the cook would make of her curiously assorted purchases and it was perhaps as well that she was not privileged to hear his comments upon them. She went upstairs to her room, sniffing contentedly at her posy. She was not disappointed; there was a roll of paper thrust down deep among the flowers. Its contents was short but very much to the point.

Arrange for Bianca, Giannina and *yourself* to go to Padua tomorrow afternoon. As long as my brother-in-law stays they won't make difficulties. Wear your hair in ringlets tonight and tomorrow morning. Tell the Wachtmeister you are expecting a singing pupil tomorrow morning for a last lesson before you leave. They will come about ten. It will be Signora Matteo and her niece, Elena. Alessandro will take the party to get the afternoon train. Burn this.

She obeyed this last instruction after she had discussed it with the Paron and then heard him announce his decision to send his wife and daughter — and the governess of course — to Padua until all this distressing affair should be over. His wife was prostrated by the event and would be better away from it all and his daughter would be a comfort to her. Later the Wachtmeister reported that this move would be permitted and preparations began for the journey.

Mary having set these in train, packed her own trunk, leaving out her old blue velvet walking dress and a hat with a thick veil which would protect her face from the smuts. That done she set tongs (borrowed from Tia Caterina) to heat on a spirit lamp. After an hour's struggle she achieved a crop of rather unruly ringlets which hung unbecomingly about her broad face. She made a disgusted grimace at her reflection and went to try the effect upon Giannina, who was already at the stage of sitting on the trunk lids to make them shut.

Mary endured her charge's strictures on the new style she had adopted and then dismissed the maid who had actually done the packing.

"Meess Maria, you can*not* ... it is not all becoming. You look ... I don't know ... blowsy ... not like yourself a bit."

"I'm aware. There's a possible reason ..."

Quickly she explained what she thought the reason might be, and how Giannina was to behave if she were right, and the girl nodded bright-eyed and excited at the prospect of such an adventure. Later they went downstairs, Mary's curls presenting an unexpectedly frivolous picture for the Wachtmeister as she mentioned the pupil she was expecting. As, on Mary's instructions, he and his men had been lavishly fed his mood was receptive ... not to say amiable. She noted that Guiseppe had not stinted on the wine. She had suggested del Collio, a potent wine. A similar repast tomorrow would, she hoped, have a similarly soporific effect.

It was a leadenfooted evening and a sleepless night. However, Mary's slumbers were disturbed less by the thought of what was to come, than by her unaccustomed curl-papers. Giannina had put them in for her, releasing the tension they both felt in a gale of giggles at the unseemly picture Mary presented. The victim searching in vain for any position on the pillow in which she would be free from those hard knobs of hair, thought incredulously of the thousands of females who nightly endured such discomfort in the cause of mere beauty. She resolved that only a matter of life and death would persuade her; she was brought up very short indeed by the memory of the Wachtmeister's face last night. This was not a mere schoolboy prank. Sobered she lay on her back and stared into dark, reviewing her arrangements ...

In the event, things went unbelievably smoothly. Her ringlets astonished by their profusion; Giannina held her excitement on a tight rein, presenting for the benefit of the soldiers the picture of a grief-stricken sister and a dutiful daughter. At ten o'clock the knocker on the front door heralded the arrival of Signora Matteo and her niece. Mary waited to greet them at the foot of the staircase while Guiseppe shuffled from the kitchen. The soldiers who, like all soldiers, had been at pains to make themselves comfortable, looked up from the collection of cane chairs with which they had created a military enclave in a corner of the hall. In that high hall it was almost cool and there was a general air of unbuttoned collar and loosened belt. The Wachtmeister who was almost asleep over a pipe, kicked the youngest recruit to his feet with a mumbled order to see who it was. Guiseppe fumbled the doors open and the morning sun struck into the cool gloom like a hammer-blow. The recruit, already bashful at such an unmilitary assignment, was too dazzled to get more than a glimpse of a vast woman in a vast hoop wearing a bonnet on which danced an assortment of flowers, feathers and fruit, which astonished even Mary who was accustomed to the Signora's taste in head-gear. His eyes fixed on this confection, the recruit barely noticed its companion, a slim, demure, rather tall young woman in a grey gown with shining black ringlets tumbling out of her old-fashioned caravan bonnet.

Mary swept forward to greet her friends and contrived to get between them and the recruit, who retreated despite some opposition from his boots to the military enclave. In response to a sleepy enquiry he answered.

"Just an old griffin with a hat ... du lieber Gott! An' a girl with her."

This party passed through the central arch to the Music Room where Giannina was waiting. She flung herself at Signora Matteo's companion.

"How could you? How could you?" she demanded passionately "Mama has been nearly out of her mind and Papa has aged ten years!"

The Signora sighed and turned to Mary.

"The scheme, my dear girl is quite simple. You are to be Elena and ..."

She bent down and rummaged under her ample skirts.

"... and she : ... is to become you!"

She surfaced rather red in the face and produced a fair wig

dressed in ringlets which had been pinned inside the cage of the crinoline. Mary stowed it away in a similar hiding place.

"I have a hat with a thick veil . . ." she began when the door opened and Tia Caterina billowed in.

"The Lieutenant is come!" she announced dramatically, "at the very instant you went under the arch he arrived. He is with the Paron in his study and is giving him the permit to travel. Doubtless he will come here!"

Mary thrust her back to the door.

"Take in wine, coffee, brandy, anything . . . try to delay him."

Tia Caterina gave her a conspiratorial look and patted her shoulder.

"Rest tranquil, Signorina, it is done. It is the best Recioto and Sylvana took it in."

Sylvana was noticeable . . . to say the least.

"Giannina! Upstairs with you, quickly. I can't trust you not to giggle. Signora, of your goodness please to be seated here and if he should come do what you can to prevent his coming *right* in."

The Signora sat herself upon a frail chair with a Horatian air and Giannina, without waiting to resent such aspersions, slipped out by a small door in the corner. Mary took 'Elena' by the arm and begged his pardon when he winced.

"Take off that bonnet."

"But . . ." he began in alarm.

"Off," said Mary. "To sing in a bonnet would rouse suspicion at once . . ."

"But I am not going to sing," he protested.

"Indeed you are."

He followed her to the piano and she placed him carefully so that his back was to the door and he masked the person seated at the keyboard.

"Clasp your hands at your waist," she told him, "and try not to look as if they belonged to someone else. Do you know 'Batti, batti, O bel Masetto'?"

"Of course I do not!" he said miserably.

"You've heard me sing it before now. I am going to sing it again. Pretend to sing . . . look at the words and mouth them. And whatever you do, keep me hidden from the doorway. Ready?"

She played the introduction to that impertinent aria and began to sing. Pietro, his eyes fixed on the score did his nervous best to mime. Mary stopped.

"Does it convince you?" she asked the Signora.

"To the ultimate!" was the encouraging reply.

They began the aria again and Pietro gained confidence as the music became more familiar. He was a little surprised when Mary faltered . . . lost the time and stopped. He was even more surprised to be scolded for faulty breathing in clear and carrying tones.

"For that phrase," said Mary, "you must hold the note, so."

She demonstrated in a harsh rather strained voice.

"Now you try."

Her voice changed to her usual effortless and creamy soprano.

"Much better."

She played the introduction again, and under cover of the firework arpeggios, muttered,

"They are just outside . . . I heard them. Remember, keep me hidden!"

He nodded, his face pale among the ridiculous ringlets and Mary launched once more into the aria. He heard the door open, a scandalised murmur from the Signora and concentrated for all he was worth on the miming. Eyes seemed to be boring into his back and he dreaded the end of the aria. It came, all too soon and there was a spatter of clapping from the door and a guttural 'Pravo! Pravo!'

"Curtsey, you fool," said Mary under cover of a crashing glissando, "Hang your head . . . look bashful, awkward . . ."

Pietro found no difficulty in obeying this command.

"My niece is so shy," announced the Signora, the every essence of aunthood, "You will have to overcome that, my dear, before you make your début. Sometimes, my dear Signor Murano, I wonder if dear Elena has the temperament, the fire for the opera."

"Of a certainty she has the voice," said the Lieutenant.

"And now," said Mary, "scales. Are you ready, Elena?"

She struck a chord.

"C major!"

The Lieutenant beat a retreat from this pedestrian occupation much to the relief of all concerned, but Mary sang scales for half an hour until at last he left the house.

After that it was time for the midday meal, and Mary saw to it that the soldiers feeding by detachments at the kitchen table should have a chance to see her bustling in and out in her blue gown and the pretty hat with the veil up. Giannina came in to bid a tearful farewell to Tia Caterina and was clucked over.

"All sensibility, the Signorina," said Tia Caterina and the kitchen unanimously shook its collective head and drew the breath between its teeth.

"The poor little one!" it chorused and turned a reproachful stare upon the current batch of soldiers who ducked their heads and ate the more. Guiseppe shook his head in agreement and absentmindedly refilled their glasses for the second time.

Upstairs Mary was exchanging clothes with Pietro. She hooked him into the blue gown and inserted some necessary wadding where the dress hung upon him despite his sulky protests. Then she settled the fair wig over his own dark hair.

"Your skin and your eyebrows are too dark."

She had darkened her own brows a trifle that morning but had not felt it wise to overdo it. Among her preparations had been the looking out of a jar of cosmetic, which La Fiorella had once used to whiten her arms. Quickly she smeared this over his face paying special attention to his eyebrows. She looked at her handiwork and nodded.

"You'll do. Now you know how to go on. Don't lift that veil whatever may happen. Giannina's waiting for you in her room. Good luck, my dear."

Back in her own room she squeezed into the grey gown which strained uncomfortably under her arms. However, the silk shawl would cover deficiencies and gapes. The black wig was very tight over her own abundant hair, but it would not be for long. She manoeuvred into the caravan bonnet, and as she peered out from the cavernous interior, she sympathised heartily with blinkered horses.

The Signora was waiting for her in the Music Room and the two of them were ushered out by Guiseppe. The soldiers hardly spared them a glance. Once in the gondola Mary asked that they should be taken to the café near the station.

"I must *know*," she explained.

The Signora looked doubtfully but agreed to this plan.

By three o'clock Mary had a headache from the tight wig and between them they had accounted for six cups of coffee. Just as they were beginning to wonder whether things had gone horribly wrong, Alessandro's gondola appeared and drew up at the station landing stage. They watched their party enter the station, 'Mary' bent solicitously over a tearful mother and daughter. They still had the barriers and checks within the station to pass. At last the fluting note of the engine announced the train's departure and Mary dared to look at her companion and smile.

"Signora, I think we have done it, I really do!"

Signora Matteo smiled back a little wanly and shifted on the uncomfortable seat.

"And now, Maria, we can go home, perhaps ... I have much lemonade with my luncheon and now so much coffee ..."

Mary stared at her.

"Home?" she queried and laughed. "You know, that was the one thing I didn't think about. Where *I* was to go ..."

She giggled.

The Signora rose and made for the cluster of gondolas at the landing-stage. Hurrying did not become one of her build but still she hurried.

"You are to come with me," she said over her shoulder, "where else?"

"But what then?" insisted Mary.

The Signora turned round and regarded her with exasperated affection. Almost she was dancing from foot to foot.

"Please," she begged, "let us discuss this in the boat."

The plan, it appeared, was that Mary should lie close at the Calle di Fuseri for a fortnight or three weeks until the hue and cry had died down. An attempt would then be made to smuggle her out of Venice and to join the family in Padua.

"Though how this smuggling may be done I do *not* know," worried the Signora the following morning. "Surely there cannot be two such women as you in all Italy."

"Could I not be disguised as a boy?" asked Mary, her face solemn.

The Signora considered her guest.

"My dear, you favour Juno and not Diana. I do not see you in the role of Fidelio. But rest content. Signor Todaro will assuredly find a way.

With that Mary was forced to be satisfied. She waited with what patience she could muster for word to come. Instead there came a parcel of blue muslin and an unsigned scrawl.

Elena's wardrobe must be limited. Occupy your unaccustomed leisure with this.

Mary regarded the material with misgiving. She appreciated the unexpected thoughtfulness which remembered that her own possessions were now near Padua. She had indeed become uncommonly weary of that tight grey confection. Moreover, the anonymous sender had chosen a colour which Mary knew to be becoming to her. On the other hand the parcel suggested a prolonged stay, which was unwelcome. She disliked the close confinement and disliked being a pensioner of the Matteos. However, dressmaking provided a much-needed occupation. For a week she stayed in the tiny garden-court of the Calle di Fuseri house and cut and stitched, with results which even she allowed to be pleasing.

Two days after the dresses were finished she was playing the piano and revolving schemes for smuggling herself into a fishing boat when another, smaller parcel arrived, again with a note.

More occupation for you [it began abruptly] in case you are thinking of learning to swim. The Comitato would be infinitely obliged if you would translate the enclosed into your impeccable Italian.

'The enclosed' was a thick wad of English and American newspaper cuttings which dealt with Italian affairs. Mary dealt with them easily enough and saw them appear in the Comitato's illegal news-sheets. In one of them there was a 'Letter from Free Italy', which was unmistakably the work of Pietro, and in which he gloated over the hoodwinking of the Occupation forces and rejoiced in the fact that no culprit had been found for the explosion at the barracks. Mary frowned over the article and reflected on the hurt he had done his own family and, not for the first time, on the young Austrians blown to bloody rags for a students' prank.

It remained oppressively hot, alleviated only by the thunderstorms, which gathered over the hills and advanced on the city like aerial armies. Mary's room became unbearable in the afternoons. She formed the habit of taking a writing-board out on to her balcony at that time. The Signora who had a living to eke out, had filled her rooms with summer visitors and Mary could venture down, black-wigged, only when the coast was clear. She was out there one afternoon when a movement at the far end of the Calle caught her eye. It was the hour of the siesta and the narrow way was usually deserted at that time. She looked at the portly figure paying off his boatman and recognised Sior Paolo. Quickly she got up and slipped back into her room, half-closing the shutters. She watched him through the louvres. He was strolling through the Calle examining the buildings as if he were a visitor. When he reached the Matteo house Mary lost sight of him under the balcony and waited for what seemed a long time. The bell pealed and Francesca leaned out from a first floor window in the charming informal style of the Venetians to cry,

"Chi xe?"

The exchange which followed confirmed Mary's suspicions.

Sior Paolo who was unknown to the Signora, represented himself as looking for lodgings. The Signora cheerfully agreed to show him the rooms which were available. This tour appeared to be exhaustive. When he took his leave, promising to let her know by the following afternoon, Mary's was almost the only room he had not explored. She felt uneasy. Sior Paolo had not come to the Calle di Fuseri by chance.

Her unease was justified later in the evening when she was sitting with the Matteos. Another unsigned note was handed in by Angelo, who now took for granted that he would be regaled with heaped plates by the Signora, whose terrifying frowns he had learned to discount within five minutes of making her acquaintance. With the Signor he conducted long precocious political discussions and interrogated that veteran on his experiences during the rising of '48 with a thoroughness which delighted the old man. The note he brought was longer than usual.

I must ask you to keep close for a day or two. The young fool P. has sent his father a letter by one of our couriers. It is unspeakably indiscreet : it gives away your part in his escape and links his father with the Comitato. His father unbelievably did not destroy it and it has disappeared. I fear for your safety. Angelo will stay. Send him for me if you have trouble !

Mary burned the note immediately. She felt trapped. The note combined with Sior Paolo's enquiries pointed to one frightening conclusion. The sooner she was out of Venice the better it would be for a number of people, the Matteos, the Muranos, del Doria and herself, of course; she had no desire to discover the inside of an Austrian jail. The question was how could this be achieved. Her mind again began to revolve round fishing boats. She turned to Angelo who was engaged in a passionate defence of the republican principle, which was none the less convincing for being based on the idea that a republic meant a state in which the governing body would include street urchins.

"Angelo, I wish to find out . . ."

She explained her scheme and he laughed at her.

"But, Signorina, this is a regular trade ... and a profitable! My cousin Giacomo he has taken many, many ... a twinkle of a lamp is all he wants. But it is rough, Signorina, very fishy ... and he can take you only to Istria and what would you do there?"

He wrinkled his nose.

"It is a barbarous land, Istria. Not for you."

"What I want you to do ..." Mary began and was then brought up short. 'A regular trade and a profitable.' Dirt or no dirt, fish or no fish, Giacomo would not provide such a service for nothing and she had little or no money left. While she was wrestling with this problem there came a ring at the bell. Francesca's 'Chi xe?' brought forth the customary but uninformative reply, 'Friends!' The Signora shooed Mary and Angelo into her bedroom and swept to the door. If it was someone ... as it might be Sior Paolo ... whom she did not wish to admit, she would be less easily overborne than Francesca.

Mary with her ear to the door recognised a welcome in the sounds from the hall and was not surprised to be summoned from her refuge to greet a familiar figure. She exclaimed with pleasure.

"Eduardo, my best of friends! How are you?"

He bowed over her hand with the grace which sat oddly on his tubby frame.

"I prosper," he told her, "even in these days I prosper. Without doubt undeservedly but there it is."

The company protested that he undervalued his deserts.

"You know, do you not that the Benedetto has reopened its doors?" he told them.

He accepted a glass of wine from the Signora who made a face at the mention of the Benedetto. Eduardo made a conciliatory gesture of his hand.

"Signora, you are right ... it is not and never will be the Fenice. The old days are gone, never to return, I fear. But it means work, Signora ... and engagements are hard to come by."

The Signor interrupted. He raised his own glass and said firmly,

"To that Day which will come."

The company drank and when they had done Eduardo fumbled in his breast pocket.

"I was paid today," he observed, and if there was a note of surprise in his voice it astonished no one present, accustomed as they all were to the vagaries of theatrical finance, "and when I was summoned to the office Umberto brought the post in . . ."

He put his finger to his nose.

"Umberto," he confided, "is of our number."

The company nodded their understanding.

"Behold," announced Eduardo producing an envelope, "he gave me this."

'This' was a letter which he handed to Mary.

"It was addressed to you and I did not wish that Carettoni should know that I knew of your whereabouts . . . so I said nothing I was silent, silent as a statue . . ."

Mary reflected with gratitude and some amusement on the effort it must have cost him.

"I do not trust that Carettoni, me," declared Eduardo his eyes darting conspiratorially round the room. "I ask myself, how is it that the theatre is again open? I ask myself, how is it that the printing press has come twice within a hairsbreadth of discovery? I can find one answer . . . one only. So, behold . . . when I see that this letter is for Meess Porretusa I put it in the innermost pocket of my coat; then I smile upon that one behind the desk and thank him for my pitiful pitttance and depart."

He put his finger to his nose again.

"And I come here by many ways and none of them straight," he assured them, "not by me will you come to harm, my friends."

He smiled upon them and drained his glass which was promptly refilled by the Signora. If she spilled a little in her anxiety to discover what it was in the letter which had turned Mary's face to the colour of chalk, it was not surprising.

Mary had examined the envelope when Eduardo handed it to

her. The sprawling hand was familiar, the postmark was Vienna...

"Flora," she had muttered, "at last..."

She had not expected her sister to conduct a regular correspondence, but the long silence since she had departed with von Fuschl had worried her. The letter was addressed to her at the Teatro Benedetto with impassioned exhortations to whomever it might concern to send it forward to wherever Mary might now reside as it was URGENT, very URGENT and IMPORTANT. Mary examined the envelope to see whether these might not have attracted the attention of the authorities, but it appeared to be untouched. She smiled at the anxiety expressed on the cover, and with a silent hope that Flora did not stand in need of money she slit open the envelope. The smile died as she read. She looked up to find the assembly staring at her with concern.

"Angelo," she said harshly and Angelo leaped to his feet at the note in her voice.

"Signorina?"

"Go," said Mary, "arrange for your cousin Giacomo to be ready for a passenger as soon as he can."

"It will be an hour after sunset," promised Angelo, "it is always thus. He will lie off the Riva del Schiavoni."

Mary looked at the frivolous French clock which palpitated the minutes away upon the Matteos' sideboard. It was a few minutes after six o'clock. Eduardo put down his glass.

"Signorina... you are in trouble. How may I help?"

Mary looked at him.

"Eduardo, I must depend upon you for a good deal."

He put his square, beautifully cared-for hand flat on his chest in a theatrical gesture which yet carried absolute conviction.

"You may," he assured her.

"You will know... where is there a fiesta in Venice today?"

She was safe in asking this. Scarcely a day passed in Venice where one parish or another did not celebrate the festival of their particular saint. Eduardo whose living was made by playing at such occasions was familiar with them all.

"In the Campo San Giacomo," he said at once.

Mary turned to Angelo.

"Tell Alessandro to be at the Campo San Giacomo in an hour. He must be ready to take someone to Giacomo's boat. Run, Angelo this is important."

Angelo with an air remniscent of Puck preparing to girdle the earth, sprang into action.

"Upon the instant," he said and was gone.

8

". . . In a foreign land!"

Lohengrin: WAGNER

IT WAS LA FIORELLA'S moment of triumph. She emerged from
the door of the chapel under an arch of swords provided by
Steiger's fellow officers, and paused for a moment to smile her
appreciation on these handsome young men, before she let her
newly acquired husband hand her up into the landau. It was
perhaps a pity that the married officers were not in evidence, but
La Fiorella did not despair of winning them (and their wives)
before too long. Vienna was not really an exclusive society as
long as the candidate for entry possessed youth, beauty and of
course money. La Fiorella planned a campaign of intimate
parties to which she could, in time, inveigle those who at present
considered von Fuschl's operatic mistress beneath their notice.
The prospective Gräfin von Fuschl was another proposition. In
the meantime they would not lack for friends — she blew them
a kiss — though from now on it would be wise to discourage their
flamboyant young women . . .

The wedding tour was to be postponed until Steiger had
finished his present duties in Vienna. She was then to be presented to Pappi and Mutti. Pappi and Mutti had refused to stir
out of the remote and ancient Schloss in which they spent all
year except the two months of the Vienna season, during which
time they opened up the dark and narrow-fronted house on the
Kaiserin Maria Theresa Strasse. Neither word nor token had
come from them barring an impassioned plea, tactfully suppressed by Steiger, that their son should remember what was due
to a family which had produced no fewer than five Knights of
the Order of the Golden Fleece. However, Flora (as she now
determined to be called), did not despair of winning them over

158

as well. Nor did Steiger who knew much more than she did of his father's susceptibility to pretty girls; a characteristic which contributed to his wife's desire to live in the country. As for Mutti, the first grandchild would induce a more conciliatory frame of mind, and the budding of that olive branch would not be very long-delayed. Flora's thickening waistline had been an important factor in bringing Steiger to the altar. He was a philoprogenitive young man and had not reacted enthusiastically to Flora's plan to go away and bring up his son in England. Her own lack of enthusiasm for it she had concealed successfully enough.

On their arrival in Vienna they had hired an apartment on the second floor of an ancient house which had known better days. Flora, delighting in the first home she had ever possessed, lavished white paint and gilding upon it and furnished the high-ceilinged elegant rooms with a dreadful conglomeration of carved mahogany and plush leavened with painted fans, artificial flowers and porcelain bibelots. To this 'nest' the landau bore back the bridal pair, where they were welcomed by the landlord with a ceremonial glass of wine. His wife had declined to appear although she had taken great pains to prepare the wedding-feast, which now awaited those young officers they had left outside the chapel. The landlord's wife was not one to let her moral scruples stand in the way of profit.

It was a gay party if a somewhat drunken one. Early in the proceedings Flora removed the more vulnerable of the bibelots to safety when a game of mess polo was mooted, a game enjoying an ephemeral popularity which involved chairs, soup spoons and an orange. The toasts became broader and more frequent and Steiger showed all the signs of making a night of it; as he said after the second bottle, this business had not much novelty for him, an observation which raised a ribald laugh among the guests, but brought a frown to the brow of his wife. Flora decided it was time she played a high card and retired to her boudoir where she lay down upon her bed, her arm across her eyes.

Steiger looked in after a while, swaying a little, to enquire when she should be out again as the party had just remembered the wedding-cake and were all agog to see her cut it. Flora, who had been wondering rather acidly if her absence had been noticed at all, lifted her arm and let it flop wearily to her side : she smiled wanly.

"I have the headache a little," she admitted, "the noise you know ... and in the circumstances ..."

Steiger in the exaggerated manner of the more or less drunk immediately became extravagantly solicitous. He tiptoed out of the room losing his balance at the door and grasping at the portieres in a manner which made his wife wince. He returned to the salon where he requested the company to be silent. As, however, he did this in a hoarse whisper and the guests were singing a lively drinking song his request was not met. A glass was put in his hand and a place made for him in the swaying circle. He resisted obstinately and twice repeated his wish for silence, the last time in a bellow which made the glasses chink and the windows rattle. His guests stared at him in a kind of hurt incredulity. He explained the situation.

"Fifi's got the headache ... delicate condition, you know. Obliged'f you'd take y'selves off. 'Nother time ... 'nother time."

However, the party did not end quite there. Flora emerged from her boudoir, having removed her rouge and applied a soupçon of blue cosmetic to shadow her eyes and bravely volunteered to cut the cake before a subdued but admiring throng. In fact her delicate aspect so worked upon one of the youngsters, who had had considerably more Tokay than was good for him, that he demanded tearfully to kiss the bride goodbye (as he put it). It was a misguided choice of phrase, which gave Steiger immediate cause for indulging in what Flora recognised with a sinking heart as one of his jealous rages. In menacing fashion he asked to be told exactly what his fellow-officers believed his bride to be. As none of them, drunk or sober, was prepared to answer such a searching question, this led to the rapid departure of all present including the young officer, who was forcibly removed by his collar band, blowing kisses.

This exeunt left Steiger flown with wine and spoiling for a fight with only Flora for an opponent. It was not a match. The encounter ended in Flora's tears, flight to her room and the playing there of her trump-card among the somewhat operatic trappings of the boudoir. Steiger responded to this natural call in a manner most soothing to her vanity but afterwards, side by side in the great mahogany bed she found that his grievance was still smouldering. He prefaced his plaint with a phrase she had come to know well.

"Know y'don't mean anything by it, Fifi, but you'll have to be more careful. Y'know how people talk."

He went on to list with spiteful animadversions on their character and appearance, everyone who had ever paid her any marked attention during their sojourn in the capital. From these he turned to the circumstances of their first meeting.

"...and then there was that damned lanky Italian... del Doria," he recalled, "you'd a notion of him, didn't you? You can't deceive me y'know... I've cut all my back teeth..."

Flora's nerves were thoroughly jangled by the evening and its aftermath, but she knew better than to let Steiger know how powerfully this mention of del Doria affected her. She yawned.

"I'd a notion about him while we were there, y'know... I was sure he'd something to do with the Comitato and the terrorists. Damned rebel. And I was right, y'know."

He laughed unpleasantly.

"I was right. We got proof at the Ministry this week. He won't be so damned supercilious when we get him in front of a firing-squad."

He was not drunk enough to tell her that this 'proof' had also incriminated her sister.

"You're joking with me," suggested Flora sleepily, "Tod... del Doria... was far too indolent to put himself out for politics. He was Italianissimo because it was the fashion..."

"I tell you," insisted her husband, "we've got written proof. A letter from a young fool he helped. An informer sent it to us."

"Why not to the government in Venice?" asked Flora, her mind, for once, working fast.

"Because we don't want those fools in Venice to use him as a witness at the trial. He's too useful."

"What trial?" murmured Flora in the manner of one who longed for sleep but was humouring her lord and master by taking an interest in his incomprehensible affairs.

"Del Doria's. Just now we've got him staked out like a goat in the jungle," said Steiger, "every move's being watched. Everyone in that Comitato will soon be arrested. We'll stamp them out once and for all."

"You mean he isn't in jail yet?"

"No," said Steiger, and laughed again. "What's more he won't stay in jail long. We've decided that a prominent execution will chase those murdering rats back to their holes and del Doria's the man they've chosen. In a fortnight he'll be rotting in some prison courtyard. Best forget him, Fifi."

Flora felt the sour vomit rise in her throat with horror. She gave no hint of this when she snuggled into his shoulder.

"Oh, I had already," she said protestingly, "but what a *grisly* affair. Funny, that ... but I'd no idea he was ... I mean I knew he was Italianissimo, but they all were, the Venetians ..."

This tactless comment on the political situation led to a lecture about the wrongheadedness of such beliefs, the ineffable benefit to Venice of Austrian rule, and how crimes committed in the mistaken cause of unity with the new and corrupt Italy deserved nothing but death ... from time to time Flora murmured sleepily,

"Yes, dear one, you are right of course ..."

At length Steiger slept. Flora, however was wide awake. She lay staring into the semi-darkness for a long time and came to a decision. She must try to warn del Doria ... as far as was possible, of course, without endangering herself. She could not possibly write direct to him. His correspondence would be intercepted and read and it would only incriminate her to write — and Steiger — she thought suddenly, for giving the plan away. As for her other acquaintances in Venice, they had fallen away as her relationship with von Fuschl ripened : the Dimonstrazione did not allow for a foothold in both camps, even for foreigners.

She could think of nobody who could or would carry a warning. Except one; her mind turned rather unwillingly upon Mary. Since her departure she had not written to Mary because she had hoped to make the anouncement of her wedding the first item of news in her letter and Steiger, as Mary had predicted, had not been so easy to persuade. There was also the question of money . . . in the circumstances, up until the day's ceremony it had been only sensible to save every stiver against a possible time when . . . and she had been afraid that if she reopened communications with her sister the first result would be a demand for money : a demand she was forced to admit would only have been just. She did not even know if Mary was still in Venice. She knew she had still been there in the spring because an officer on leave had seen her, painting a canal scene. After long and painful cogitation Flora was forced to the conclusion that Mary presented her only chance to warn del Doria without implicating herself. The possibility that she might implicate Mary she did not consider. She decided to send the letter to the theatre with a plea to forward it and then put the matter out of her mind altogether. She would have done her best and to worry unduly over what she could not help would harm the baby.

The decision once taken she began to consider how it could be implemented. How would she be able to send a message without arousing Steiger's suspicions and still have it arrive in time? She knew from Steiger, who still dealt with Venetian affairs at the Ministry, that the post for Venice left Vienna in the very early morning. And she could not afford to waste a single day. What was it Steiger had said, 'In a fortnight he'll be rotting . . .' She shuddered slightly. If the letter was to catch the post it must be written at once. The Austrian posts were notoriously slow.

Steiger was deeply and noisily asleep. She moved gradually away from him, pulling down the bedclothes where she had lain so that he would not feel her absence at once. Some lights from the street lamps filtered through the shutters, enough for her to find her dressing-gown and slip out of the room without making a clatter. She shut the door with immense care and tiptoed away in the direction of the salon which looked and smelt unbearably sordid. Beyond it was a small room which she had called the study, though it was seldom used for that purpose. In there was a desk, pen and paper. The gas flame lit with a soft plop which sounded to her nervous ears like an explosion which could rouse the whole neighbourhood. She listened anxiously but there was no wakeful sound from their bedroom. Almost, she decided not to risk the warning . . . suppose Steiger found out? It would not be a good beginning to their married life. Then she remembered Todaro and shuddered again at the thought of his lying dead.

The letter took some time to write. Literary composition was not Flora's forte and she had a good deal to explain which was complicated. By the time she was finished the sky was beginning to lighten in the east and sounds from below indicated that the landlady was already astir. Flora sealed and addressed the letter and from her carefully gathered hoard she took a gold coin. She tied her gown about her, tidied her hair as well as she could with her fingers and tiptoed back across the landing past the bedroom, where Steiger gave audible and rhythmic assurance that he was still asleep.

Downstairs the landlady was bustling about in a wrapper and the smell of coffee and rolls filled the kitchen. The slovenly daughter was on her knees by the hearth. Mother and daughter looked up in astonishment at the figure of Flora in the doorway. They had become accustomed to her sleeping until noon.

"Is there something the matter?" asked the mother sharply.

Flora shook her head.

"I could not sleep," she explanied, "it was so hot and after all the excitement of yesterday . . . I wrote to my sister in Venice. She should know about my wedding. I would have written before but . . ."

She looked down at the letter in her hand. Flora had no illusions concerning her landlady's opinion of her. That moralist sniffed, but there was a gleam of sympathy in her cold grey eye.

"I wondered . . . would Gretl take it to catch the morning post for me. She shall have this for her trouble."

The gleam brightened at the sight of the gold and Gretl, who in her turn had no illusions about her mother, leaped to her feet and took the letter and the gold piece. She began to untie her apron and smooth back her hair with a dirty hand.

"Willingly Fraulei . . . gnädige Frau. I will just have time."

Gretl clattered out of the room in her wooden shoes and vanished in the direction of the Post Office, glad to escape into the early morning streets. Flora thanked the landlady and returned at length to bed. To Steiger's sleepy enquiry she returned a conventional and as it chanced, a true, answer. The privy was underneath the staircase on the first floor.

*   *   *

Angelo slammed the outer door behind him and for a moment or so nobody spoke.

"It is bad news?" asked the Signora.

"Evidently," came the response from her husband, "it declares itself. Maria, you have only to say how we can be of assistance."

By way of reply she put the letter before them.

"You'd best read this before I burn it."

The two grey heads bent over the ill-written pages and Eduardo manoeuvred behind them for a view.

Vienna
Thursday.

Dearest Mary,

My dear Steiger and I were married today. I hope you will be pleased with this. He has later given me a piece of disturbing intelligence. He has duties with the Ministry here which deal with Venetian Matters. They have a Letter which tells them that that Signor Del Doria who you may remember it was his pendent I left for you is a member of the Committo Venitto or some such thing and has been active against the Austrians. Mary, I hardly like to write this they mean to _Shoot him_. He is to be watched to find the rest of this Committo and they are all to be arrested and Todaro to be shot within the week as an example not to hate the Austrians, tho I cannot see how this will do such a thing.

At first I did not believe him because it seemed strange that Todaro would be in with such a set of people he did not seem that kind. But I am convinced that it is True. I did not discover to my dear husband how distressed I was at this intelligence but dissembled I fear till I found opportunity to write in the hope that you will warn him in Time for him to make His Escape. I cannot *bear* that he should be killed because I did have a great Kindness for him.

Please I beg you burn this letter because I am anxious that Steiger does not discover My Hand in This or he will be Very Angry and I have *no one* I can turn to here in Vienna. I suppose it is Disloyal in me to work this way behind his back and not the Part of a True Wife but I have a Great Kindness to Todaro and he must not be shot. Politics make my Head ache.

I hope you are in good health my dear Mary and find suitable employment. I was surprised to hear you were in Venice still. I thought you back in the fogs and damps. I hope soon to make you an Aunt! Imagine that! I will write again very soon and hope to hear from you but beg that you will make *no mention of this* in yours if you love,

your affektionate sister,

Flora.

PS If you have comfortable news for me mention Constanze and the *Entführung*; if not best to say nothing.

F von F.

"It is unfortunate that your feather-brained sister put no date upon this!" exclaimed the Signor, "How can we know how long it has been on the way. It could be three days or it could be ten."

"Knowing the posts," said Eduardo, "most likely ten."

"No time to waste whichever it is," said Mary setting light to the letter from the embers in the brazier and watching it crumble into ashes. "Eduardo, my friend, much must depend on you. Can you find Signor del Doria?"

"If not, I know those who can. Within an hour I can be in his presence," he assured her.

"If he is not already in the New Prisons . . ." the Signora put in in her most tragic tones. Her husband shook his head at her.

"Find him, tell him what is in this letter so that all the people involved can be warned, and then ask him to meet me in the Campo San Giacomo as soon as he can . . . what is the name of the café there?"

"Ricardo's."

"At Ricardo's within the hour."

Eduardo nodded, his eyes bright.

"All this I will do and anything else that is needed. Behold me."

He kissed Mary's hand.

"This is not quite a surprise, you know," he told her, "we have been told there is a coup preparing. The Comitato is warned and some have gone already. Signor Murano joined the family in Padua last week. But of this design upon del Doria we had none of us any notion."

He gripped the hand he held.

"I must bid you farewell; good luck go with you, dear girl," he said rapidly and Mary saw the tears standing in the brown eyes. "At least I have been privileged to help you."

He kissed her hand again and left at once. Before the people who remained could move or speak he was back.

"I remember something which may be of assistance," he said, his head round the door, "this Fiesta . . . it is to be a maschera."

He disappeared again and the front door banged behind him.

"Ah!" said the Signora and she set herself at the stairs like a horse at a fence.

Mary looked at the Signor. He smiled at her and patted her arm.

"It is not so long since she and I tasted the pleasures of an older and gayer Venice, Signorina. We still have the garments in which we attended the Carnival and the fiestas when they were in very truth fiestas and not the pale imitation we know today."

The Signora appeared on the landing, a purple domino

hanging on one arm and a blue one on the other. Two white mascheras, the half-masks favoured by the Venetians dangled from her fingers.

"Doubtless it was a Providence which enjoined upon me to keep them! Come, Maria ... I will secure your hair beneath a hat of Enrico's. It must be Fidelio for you after all!"

She swept down the staircase her arms full of gleaming silk.

"Though in this case you rescue your lover *before* he is in jail ..."

Mary wondered uneasily what the Signora had guessed of her feelings where del Doria was concerned but she did not labour the point. In her room she removed the hoop from beneath her muslin skirts and assumed the blue silk cloak with its wide hood. Her head gear proved a complication, being a disguise upon a disguise. She could not appear without the black wig which covered her own well-known and easily recognisable yellow hair. On the other hand black ringlets did not consort with the Signor's broadbrimmed hat. If she tucked them into the crown of the hat the combination of her own hair and the wig made the hat balance precariously on the top of her head. She came downstairs and demanded that the Signora should cut off her own hair.

This provoked a chorus of protest worthy of a matter of more moment in Mary's eyes. The Signora, with the aid of a hairnet which might have held fast a dolphin and a stout shoelace, succeeded in restraining the fair hair under the black wig and then tied the black ringlets in the nape of Mary's neck. In the dark (a threat of thunder was darkening the sky into an early twilight), with the hood of the cloak rolled high behind her head and the hat pulled well down, Mary, it was decided at last, might just pass for a man if no one examined her salient points too closely. The Signor, when she was paraded before him, tugged at his chin and shook his head a little doubtfully,

"Superb," he commented, "magnificent ... but unmistakably feminine ..."

If Mary felt a little like a skinned hare after such treatment, she thought it would be ungracious to mention it.

By the time her costume was complete she had less than half an hour to reach the Campo San Giacomo. Angelo had returned, his errands successfully discharged, ready to guide her through the maze of calli. Mary bundled the remaining maschera and domino into a carpet-bag and donned her own mask. She was about to make her grateful farewells to the Matteos when the doorbell jangled imperatively. Francesca who had been watching the proceedings critically raised the window in the hall and gave her usual cry. Before she had her reply she jerked her head back in and exclaimed her voice sharp with alarm,

"Soldiers, Paron ... soldiers! Ten or a dozen of them and with guns."

The party retreated quickly to the kitchen. Angelo tugged at Mary's cloak.

"Could you climb a little, Signorina? You are tall and strong and it would not be difficult I promise you ..."

Mary nodded.

"Then come," said Angelo urgently, "they will not have people at the back because they think there is no way out. But I know of one. Come."

There was no time for more than a hurried kiss on the Signora's plump cheek. In a flurry of passionate good wishes Angelo and Mary slipped out into the garden-court. Meanwhile the Matteos began to conduct a campaign of delay; first of all from the window they demanded to know the soldiers' business severally and together and failed to hear the answers. The discussion then adjourned to the tiled hall, when the arrivals showed signs of preparing to break down the door. What, the Signora demanded to be told, brought such a ruffianly crew to a respectable house? If they were looking for food and drink there were many low tavernas at which they could be suitably entertained. If they were looking for women, she told them, they had best return to Austria for no respectable Venetian would be seen with a white uniform and none but respectable women ever entered the doors of her house.

"You might say we were looking for a woman," interrupted the corporal in charge with a grin, "she is large, yellow-haired and blue-eyed : calls herself English and has an English passport. Her name is Porretusa, Maria Porretusa . . . and she is wanted for questioning in connection with the escape of a terrorist prisoner."

The Signora's look of blank incomprehension was masterly and to be equalled only by that on the face of her husband. They exchanged bewildered glances across the hall.

"Porretusa? Porretusa! Ah!"

Their faces became joint studies in dawning intelligence.

"Of course!" exclaimed the Signora.

"Of course!" echoed her husband, "You must mean La Fiorella."

It was the turn of the corporal to look bewildered.

"She was the diva at the Teatro Benedetto," explained the Signora, "she lodged here with us for some months about a year ago. Is that not correct, Papa?"

Papa nodded wisely.

"That is correct, my angel. You have the name wrong, my friend. Her name was Fiorella, not Maria but I saw the other name . . . what was it, Porretusa on her passport."

The corporal frowned and consulted his warrant.

"The name here," he said obstinately, "is Maria . . ."

"But you are come too late . . ." boomed the Signor edging up to him, "La Fiorella is gone to Vienna some six months and more since."

By this time he was near enough to the corporal to nudge him painfully in the ribs.

"And," he added behind his hand, "she went there with one of your officers . . . she was his . . . little friend, you know . . ."

He nudged the corporal again and winked enormously.

The corporal regained his balance, folded up his paper and confronted the Signora.

"My orders are to search," he told her.

Her shoulders heaved in a shrug.

"With my goodwill," she exclaimed, "I have no girl here. There is my niece Elena but she has returned to her mother in

Malamocco for a short time. She will be back in a week if you wish to see her. But the Signorina Porretusa is not here."

"Ah, Mama!" said Signor Matteo with the air of one who had made a shattering philosophical discovery, "it has just occurred to me . . . if this young man could but let us know when he finds Signorina Porretusa, perhaps we could at last return the baggage she left with us . . ."

He turned again to the corporal and became oppressively confidential.

"La Fiorella left us suddenly, you understand. There was an incident at the theatre I believe and she was one with a temperament, that one. These divas . . ."

He sighed and his wife snorted her indignation at such an aspersion.

"Divas! I could tell you a tale or two about the opera, me! And they would concern the tenors and the basses . . . not the divas alone. I can remember . . ."

She began on a tale of a diva and a tenor and an egg pressed into the hand during a pathetic aria and again the Signor winked.

"I tell you I have to search the house," insisted the corporal interrupting the story without consideration and making the Signora stand aside. He nodded to the men who had been listening open-mouthed to this masterly performance, and they followed him up that graceful staircase, looking singularly out of place.

The Matteos made no further protest. By this time Francesca would have had time to bundle Mary's scanty possessions into a bag and remove the used bedding from the top-floor room : and if Mary and Angelo had not managed to climb the wall of the courtyard by now they never would. Besides to delay the search longer would be suspicious in itself. The Signora, however, had one more gambit in hand. Francesca had been asked to lock every room not occupied. The keys had been placed in a drawer and after they had been found (the corporal threatened to break down the doors with musket butts if they were not), she took them out of the drawer in such a panic that the frayed string on which they were threaded caught and broke, so that all the keys were out of order and the corporal had to wait while she tried several keys in each lock.

The four lodgers who were in residence at this point were naturally not locked in, but they tended to be indignant at this intrusion into their holiday and argumentative about having their possessions disturbed by a search. This was particularly true of the Americans in the appartmente signorile who made bitter and prolonged animadversions about the ways of tyranny in a benighted Europe, most of which were lost upon the soldiers as they were in American. Even the Signor with his wide knowledge of English was unable to understand some of the phrases used. The encounter, as was inevitable when the protagonists understood not a word of one another's language, was prolonged and heated. In fact by the time the soldiers left with nothing but a carpet-bag containing La Fiorella's clothes to show for their search. Mary was already explaining to del Doria her plan for his escape.

9

"Before we leave these haunts!"

Faust: GOUNOD

WHILE THE MATTEOS WERE enjoying themselves in this fashion (and it may be said that they enjoyed the drama immensely both then and later), Mary and Angelo were threading their way through a maze of alleys and passages and tiny tank-like courtyards. Mary had proved herself more athletic than Angelo expected, and made nothing of climbing the magnolia-tree in the corner and stepping from that on to the mossy coping of the wall. She had balked slightly at the drop on the other side, the more as there seemed to be no exit from the minute courtyard of which the wall made one side. However she was shamed by Angelo's offer to catch her and told him to stand aside before she lowered herself as far as she could and then dropped.

"I had no time to waste chipping you out of the pavement!" she replied breathlessly to Angelo's reproaches when she landed awkwardly and pitched sideways. He burst into peals of laughter at this notion and was still laughing when he led her through a door without even the ceremony of knocking, and greeted the baker who was hard at work within, with his arms up to the elbow in the bread-trough. He gave a brief greeting, nodded curiously at Angelo's masked companion and continued with his kneading. They left by another door which gave on to a narrow alley. Angelo led her twisting and turning through obscure openings and arches. The alleys stank of kitchen refuse and worse, cats materialised out of the shadows, startled faces peered from doorways, and once a raucous female voice from four storeys above accused Mary of being on the run from an injured husband, a suggestion which made Angelo giggle again in a manner not at all becoming to one in flight from the law. Even Mary smiled, preoccupied as she was with the possibility that she was even then too late.

They paused to get back their breath and their sobriety at the mouth of a dark passage which gave on to a small campo. Here the business of the evening had begun. Hawkers cried their wares, an old woman with fluffy white hair and a scarcity of yellow fangs conducted a monotonous quarrel with a vast black-clad female.

"Beast!" cried the old woman.

"Thou!"

"Fool!"

"Thou!"

"Liar!"

"Thou!"

Two girls were exchanging intimate details of their private lives from two upper windows three houses apart. On the far side of the Campo glinted a canal, and there was a gondolier sitting on a bollard plucking a guitar and singing 'La Biondina in Gondoleta' in a hoarse baritone. From the ancient church came the sound of chanting and a procession of whitegowned girls and acolytes in grimy lace were escorting a tiny yellowish wooden statue down the church steps. Lanterns were strung across the Campo ready for the darkness which was already gathering in the corners. Angelo pulled at her cloak.

"There's Ricardo's," he said and indicated a café on the far side of the square. "Seat yourself to the left where the light is dim. I will go tell Alessandro you are ready. He is at the Goldoni Bridge. He will wait there."

He jerked his chin at the fondamente where the gondolas clustered waiting for custom. Mary nodded agreement.

"In half an hour," she said, "it will be dark by then ... he should be ready to go out on to the Canalazzo ..."

To turn a gondola in the narrowest waterways was a difficult sometimes an impossible task.

"Depend upon us," said Angelo and melted back into the darkness like one of the omnipresent cats.

Mary pulled the brim of the hat down over her face and

prayed that all her arrangements were not in vain and that the Austrians had not arrested del Doria already. She strode man-fashion into the Campo, her heart beating hard and a prickle of sweat under her arms. If the Austrians had sprung their trap she could be walking right into it.

Ricardo's was not yet busy. A waiter came over within minutes of her sitting down at the dimly lit table.

"Behold me," he said incuriously and swiped at the table with a grimy napkin.

Mary remembered only just in time to deepen her voice and ordered a glass of sugar-and-water. She sipped this uninspiring concoction. The procession formed and then started to move around the square, so that the little statue could inspect every corner of his domain. Gradually the inhabitants emerged from their doors and joined the procession. There was no sign of a familiar tall figure and Mary's heart sank into her shoes. The chanting followers of the statue increased in number, until the glittering cross born by the parocco and the sweating statue-bearers had almost caught up with the disreputable 'tail' of beggars, lasagnoni and urchins. Still there was no sign of del Doria. The statue passed by the café and Mary crossed herself in salutation, scattering a handful of soldi into the hammered bronze plate, which was carried by a couple of acolytes, ob-viously chosen by the parroco for their appeal being small, waif-like and, as with almost all Venetian children, heart-rendingly beautiful.

From the following crowd a tall figure separated itself and slipped into the chair beside her. She felt an uprush of utter relief which prevented her from speaking for a moment, and realised how piercingly anxious she had been. Even if she had been able to say anything it was doubtful if he could have heard it, for the band which had been gathering as player after player hurried up with his instrument under his arm attained a quorum and broke into a loud and doleful march. The waiter standing napkin in hand as if he were taking the salute at a march-past of prospective customers was in no hurry to attend to the new-comer.

"Did Eduardo tell you about the letter?" Mary enquired very quietly when the band had retired a little way.

Del Doria nodded.

"I knew there was something in the wind," he replied, "I've been expecting something of the kind ever since that letter disappeared . . ."

"You should have gone."

"There was still work to finish," he shrugged.

"But you'll go now?"

"My usefulness is over," he told her. "I can do more from Italy now. *If* I can get there."

He ordered wine from the hovering waiter and waited until he was out of earshot again.

"What do you propose?" he asked.

Mary explained quickly and he nodded agreement. They fell silent when the wine arrived.

"I drink to you," he said, raising his glass, "Maria the imperturbable!"

She blushed and raised her glass in turn.

"To your safe journey."

Under cover of the deepening darkness he took her hand and kissed it for the third time and for the third time Mary tried to distract herself from the effects of this commonplace gesture by considering his political motives.

"To *our* safe journey," he corrected her, "you will have to come too. If you stay they will put you in jail, and your Consul will have the devil's own job to persuade them that you are an innocent British traveller."

"I know," Mary agreed, "I am afraid to stay longer."

Del Doria raised his eyebrows at such an admission.

"Soldiers came to the Calle di Fuseri just as I left," she explained, "I am more than uneasy about the Matteos."

His amused expression vanished at this news.

"I couldn't bear that they should suffer for sheltering me."

"As long as you are not found there," he reassured her, "I doubt if they will do more than search. If they do . . . well, we are not entirely without influence yet."

"Alessandro will be here soon," said Mary, "I have a domino for you . . . we must hurry."

"There is a room inside," he said, "Ricardo is to be trusted."

Inside the proprietor responded to del Doria's muttered request by nodding at a door in the back wall of the café. Once inside the little, barely furnished room Mary produced the domino and the mask.

"I thought perhaps, a little maquillage . . ." she suggested, "Bend down a trifle."

Swiftly she applied a white cosmetic to the wings of black hair on his temples and combed it in evenly. It made a surprising difference to his appearance. He peered at the flyblown mirror by the light of the one candle.

"An elderly stranger," he commented and swung the purple silk round his shoulders. The mask was fastened and so was Mary's and they went out into the café. The rickety door jammed for a few seconds and Mary's heart pounded with panic. It gave after a push and they joined a crowd of fiesta-goers in dominos and masks who had arrived while they were in the inner room.

"Does no one in this city ever repair anything?" she grumbled under her breath as he steered her to the door.

"And I hoped you were in a fair way to becoming a Venetian," he remarked lightly, "surely you realise that for two thousand years the Venetians have expected their city to sink into the sea, if not today, why then tomorrow or the next day. What use to mend anything which is certain to be engulfed. Indeed . . ."

He peered out of the door at the Campo.

". . . to repair anything is to invite disaster . . . don't you understand . . . just as to water your garden is to invite a thunderstorm."

In the square the lanterns were being lit by an urchin with a taper who stood upon his father's shoulders. In the centre of the Campo on chairs borrowed from the café sat the band which had accompanied the saint upon his annual airing. The procession coiled into a tableau in the centre of the square by the well-curb. The music died and the parroco asked a blessing on the parish for another twelve months. The parishioners dropped on to their knees and called out to the statue the particular favours they wished he would do for them in the coming year. An acolyte spattered them generously with holy water. The parroco blessed the assembly again and dismissed them to celebrate the day. He and his entourage turned towards the steps of the church, the statue bobbing and swaying in their midst, and the band broke into a dance tune as soon as they disappeared into the gloomy interior. The little statue's outing was over for another year.

The band thumped away industriously and all round the square dancers rotated solemnly in the Furlana. Around the dancers was a ring of onlookers, old men and women, cake-sellers, fruit-sellers, women with solemn babies and everyone who could, tapping out the rhythm. The return of the statue did not take long because in a few minutes the white-gowned girls were among the dancers and the parroco in the black soutane of every-day was sampling wine with his cronies in the café. A group of masked figures came into the square from the Salizzeria. Mary and del Doria slipped out and followed them right into the heart of the watching crowd. There was a powerful smell of wine, unwashed bodies and fried food. Mary's arm was tugged from behind and she turned in alarm to see a dark-eyed girl with greasy coarse hair and a stained velvet dress over a vast hoop. A prostitute, Mary thought, you hear of such things but how seldom you understand what it means : the brassy invitation in those dark eyes shocked her for a moment and then she smiled. After all, there could be few women who had been given just that kind of invitation. She shook her head emphatically and turned away, careful to keep the domino closed over her muslin skirts. They edged their way towards the fondamente.

Suddenly del Doria's hand clenched on her arm just above the elbow.

"Behold!" he said under his breath.

A file of white-uniformed soldiers came out of the Calle immediately opposite and marched across the Campo, regardless of the merrymakers. They were brought to a slovenly halt. Men were sent running to stand guard at each of the exits of the square.

"Stopping the boltholes," remarked del Doria.

The Wachtmeister and half a dozen men vanished into the café leaving a couple outside, enduring the loud and full-flavoured speculation as to what the soldiers were up to inside. Other more direct observations on military habits and propensities came hurtling out of the emboldening darkness.

"Alessandro isn't here, yet." Mary whispered.

"Time enough, he'll come," said her escort but under the mask his mouth looked a trifle grim.

"Why do you think the soldiers have come?"

"At a guess I would say that Eduardo was no more than a jump ahead of the warrant," del Doria speculated, "and someone has seen me coming here."

"What will they do now?"

"I wish I knew."

While they were talking the crowd had become abusive at this interruption, but their shouts were drowned by the musicians, who resumed their playing and blasted out a tarantella calculated to distract the attention of the crowd from the unfortunate sentries to the wildly gyrating figures in the centre of the square. For this the parroco might have been responsible; he was certainly near the band when it began to play. In a very short time the whole square was filled with whirling, stamping dancers; even those who were watching were jigging about from sheer delight in the wild rhythm. Out of the corner of her eye Mary saw the steel prow of a gondola nose out of the waterway between the houses, its lantern unlit, and come to a halt a boat's length and more behind the other craft. It was almost certainly Alessandro. Todaro had seen him too. He grabbed Mary's hands and they whirled with the other dancers across the paving to the other side of the square. There he took her by the waist and whisked her into the shadows, just as other maskers were doing all round the Campo. Once again they were on the edge of the crowd but this time they were right beside the water.

From the other side there was a volley of shouted orders and a clatter of boots.

"Barca! Barca!" came a hoarse whisper.

Alessandro had moved forward softly till he was right under their feet. The tide was low and the water over a metre below the fondamente. Todaro took Mary under her arms and lowered her into the gondola as if she were a featherweight. He jumped down himself, landing so softly that cockleshell craft hardly rocked.

"Back!" he called softly and urgently to Alessandro, "Go back in between the houses . . . as quickly as you like . . ."

The gondolier obeyed, his oar dipping and twisting almost without a splash. His passengers crouched on the benches their eyes on the edge of the fondamente. The boat glided backwards into the narrow space between the blind windows and the crumbling walls and there came almost imperceptibly to a halt. As they looked towards the lights and movement on the Campo they saw the silhouette of a musket just where the canal came into the square. They had not had more than a second or two to spare. Alessandro backed further in until they could hear little of the noise and music from the fiesta.

"No way through there," said Alessandro very softly, "but there is another way to the Canalazzo. Low and narrow, not easy. Not many use it."

Todaro murmured a question and Alessandro replied with a string of names which meant nothing to Mary. It was agreed to try his route and the gondolier backed his boat until the narrow channel merged into a wider one and he could turn round.

"Stay under the hood," he advised them, "this is not a way I would choose to take passengers."

Mary never forgot that silent, twisting voyage in the dark. Alessandro knew the backwaters of his city as well as his young brother knew the passages and alleys. He seemed to be able to see in the dark, for he threaded his way quickly and accurately with no more light than that shed by an occasional oil lamp above a house door or the glimmer of a taper burning before a corner shrine. At last they came out from beneath an arch so low that the steel prow had more than once brushed sparks from the stonework, into a broad waterway where the twinkling lights of other gondolas bobbed in the conflicting wakes. Todaro crawled forward to light the little lantern on the foredeck in case they should not be seen by the other boats.

Alessandro eased out into the mainstream towards the bridge they could see outlined by its lamps cross the waterway before it joined the Canalazzo. There was a bobbing cluster of lights just at one side of this bridge, but at first this did not alert them as gondolas often gathered there waiting for custom. In fact it was not until a warning shout came from the crown of the bridge that they realised there was a boom stretched across the water under the bridge, logs strung end to end upon a rope cable. They were waved into the shore where soldiers with storm lanterns were examining another gondola from stem to stern while its occupants expostulated on the quayside.

"No use to turn back," said Alessandro in an undervoice, "they'll suspect at once if we do. We'll have to bluff . . ."

Mary had a sudden idea. She pushed the mask up on her forehead, pulled off the hat and loosened the curls of her wig. Then she removed the blue domino and rumpled up her muslin dress.

"They'll want to know why we're wandering about the canals at this hour," she said very quietly, "and we'll show them a reason. Alessandro, we're bound for the Piazza as slowly and as roundabout as you can manage . . . you can be bored with us if you think that will help. And you . . ."

She turned to Todaro.

"You can have your attentions very fully engaged. Put your mask on your forehead like mine . . . it's almost as good a disguise as wearing it the usual way. Take off your cloak and your coat."

He obeyed without question and she reflected that he had none of the usual masculine amour propre which could have led to argument.

"Now unbutton your shirt and ruffle your hair. Good. You look as if you had spent the whole night in dalliance."

She was rearranging the leather cushions of the bench upon

the deck. When she had made a sort of couch of them she sat down on it and unbuttoned her high collar.

"Do you think," she asked diffidently, "you could pretend to make violent love to me?"

Alessandro gave a delighted laugh and Todaro lowered his long frame on to the cushions beside her.

"I should find it extremely difficult," he replied.

Mary was too taken aback by this apparent lack of gallantry to notice an odd note in his voice.

"It wouldn't need to be for very long," she explained apologetically, "just long enough to put them off the scent. You see this way, if they're sympathetic they might not make us get out and stand up. It's our size which will give us away."

"Alessandro!" Todaro called through the leather hood to the stern as the lanterns beckoned them to come in to the fondamente. "You are playing Cupid . . ."

Alessandro choked slightly.

". . . to my Vulcan. Tell them so."

"Understood," said the gondolier and sent the craft gliding alongside with one stroke of his oar.

Todaro put his arm over Mary and pressed her back on to the leather cushions and then bent right over her so that his face was right beside hers.

"I meant," he whispered against her ear, "that I would find it difficult to pretend . . ."

The gondola bumped against the quay. Above them Alessandro replied to questions in harsh German-Italian.

"Oh, we are supposed to be going to the Piazza . . ." he told them irritably, "but twice I have landed at the Pontili San Marco and twice he's told me to go round by this way and that . . ."

The soldiers guffawed.

"All found money for you," they said, "why grumble?"

Alessandro spat into the water.

"Not so much as a stop at a café for a glass of wine," he said, "just round and round . . ."

The next question was not audible to the couple in the shelter, and they were, in any event, otherwise occupied, but they did hear Alessandro give vent to a salacious chuckle.

"What's going on in there? Look for yourselves!" he said, "I don't care even to guess, me!"

"Don't worry," said the questioner, and stepped down into the craft so that it rocked alarmingly, "we'll keep you well-informed!"

Todaro raised his head for a second,

"I'll have to live up to Alessandro's promise," he whispered, "forgive me if I seem a trifle . . . rough . . ."

Mary then found herself grabbed in a rib-cracking embrace and her gown ripped off her shoulder. Her immediate and instinctive reaction was to struggle against such coercion, and she had already stiffened herself, when she realised that this might not present a convincing picture of waterborne lovers who had had two hours to sort out their problems. She relaxed and returned the embrace as enthusiastically as she could with one arm pinned uncomfortably under Todaro's chest. Lamplight flickered into the shelter and there was a salacious guffaw. Del Doria sat up, his mask high on his forehead and his shirt unbuttoned almost to the waist.

"What's the meaning of this?" he asked querulously. "Can't a man enjoy the company of his wife during a fiesta without the military sticking its face into his concerns."

There was a roar of laughter at this and a number of faces peered into the shelter, grinning with glee as they took in the scene. Mary gave a little squeak of dismay and pulled down the mask over her face. She sat up and pulled the torn muslin over her shoulder, while the company noted the disorder of her skirts and reported it to those who could not see.

"His wife! He says she is his wife!"

"I should have such a wife!"

"A likely story, friend!"

The first soldier made way for another who peered in, gave a low whistle of approval and withdrew to give place to a third.

"This is intolerable," scolded del Doria, "I will complain to the Commandant."

"We are sorry, Signor, to disturb you and your good lady," said the first soldier, reappearing in the entrance to the shelter, "but we are looking for a criminal . . . however, I doubt if you and your . . . wife . . . fill the bill."

He withdrew.

"Pass this lot, Adolf . . . open the boom. Can't disturb love's young dream, eh?"

He dropped the leather curtain and they felt the boat rock as he made his way round to the stern.

"You going up to the Pontili San Marco again?" he asked Alessandro.

"Yes, Corporal . . . and probably again and again after that," grumbled Alessandro.

"I'll go with you. I'm going off duty. I want to go to the Guidecca. Can you take me?"

"They would not care where I go as long as I never get there," Alessandro bitterly. "I'll take you to the Ponte dell'Accademia. Will that suit?"

"Admirably."

The back of the leather shelter bulged as the corporal sat down with his back to it.

"There are two more booms," he mentioned, "I'll frank you through. Save disturbing your lovebirds in there."

Alessandro pushed off from the fondamente and out under the bridge through the narrow space between boom and quay.

Inside the shelter Todaro lowered Mary on to the cushions again.

"It would seem that the play must go on," he breathed in her ear, "a pity to disappoint our public."

But Mary pushed his arm aside and sat up, pulling her domino over her torn dress. It was too dark for him to see her expression but the shake of her head was emphatic, not to say panicky. He put his arm round her shoulders and gave her a hug.

"Don't worry, little one, you're safe enough . . ."

The use of that inappropriate adjective was enough to revive Mary's sense of humour and restore her equilibrium. She chuckled very softly, a sound which inspired the corporal to dig Alessandro in the leg, jerk his thumb at the shelter and wink.

"You don't need to tell me that, Signor."

To her surprise this unexceptional answer seemed to make him angry. His grasp on her tightened and he almost hissed in her ear.

"And what makes you so certain? Do you underestimate me? or undervalue yourself?"

He pulled her roughly across his knees and kissed her again hard and long. Mary struggled momentarily but only to free her arms in order to return the embrace.

"Either way," he murmured after a while, "you are wrong."

Mary said nothing. The situation was beyond her experience and her habit then was to wait on events. Todaro took her chin in his hand and pushed it up.

"Do you imagine a few extra inches make you into a ... a ... monster?" he demanded.

"On occasion," she said calmly, "one is given that impression."

"Have I given it?"

"The reverse, Signor ..."

She chuckled again.

"But then you are something of a monster yourself, are you not?"

"Wasp," he said appreciatively and let her sit up again as the gondola slid to a halt at the second of the blocks. A hail from the soldier and they were away again almost without a check.

The next check was at the Ponte dell'Accademia and again the corporal vouched for them before he disembarked. The gondola rocked violently as he jumped ashore with a word of thanks and a final comment.

"Best find them a bed and then perhaps you'll be able to go sleep in yours ..." he advised.

Alessandro agreed with feeling and then manoeuvring through the gap in the boom, turned the little craft into the middle of the canal as if he were making for the Pontili San Marco. No point in making the corporal suspicious by going somewhere else. Out in midstream they all heaved a sigh of relief and began to talk.

"A near one, Signor, a very near one! I thought we would cock up our toes at that bridge. A stroke of brilliance, Signorina . . ."

"She is a woman in a thousand, Alessandro. I know of only one thing which can disturb her composure . . ."

He ignored the questioning sound which Alessandro made and bent his attention to demonstrating his knowledge to Mary. He was interrupted.

"Signor . . . would you go forward and put your hat over the lamp three times."

Todaro obeyed. A light low down on the water nearly a quarter of a mile away was raised and lowered three times in reply.

"It is clear to approach," said Alessandro, "the guard-boat must have passed. The tide is with us. Put out the lamp if you will, Signor . . . no need to advertise our presence."

Once out of the Canalazzo and on the more exposed waters of the Canale San Marco, they began to feel the waves kicked up by the off-shore breeze. Gondolas are strictly for inland waterways and Mary began to feel a trifle nervous at the plunging of the little craft. She folded up the discarded dominos and the masks and put them into the carpet bag. Her torn dress she tucked into the sleeve of her petticoat, and because the hat would not go into the now bulging bag she put it on again. It would not do to leave any trace of their occupation in Alessandro's boat. Del Doria remained outside the shelter evidently on the look out for any boat which might challenge them. Mary tidied the leather cushions and wondered with a slight shiver whether she had dreamed that episode upon them. The circumstances had been . . . peculiar; she resolved that she would behave as if it had not taken place, unless Todaro himself . . .

The gondola rubbed softly alongside the fishing boat which had proclaimed its presence unmistakably downwind for two hundred metres. There was a muffled hail.

"Chi xe?"

Mary was reminded of the Matteos' Francesca and wondered

if a little basket might come down on the end of a string to receive their card as was the custom.

"Friends of Sior Antonio Rioba," Alessandro called back.

"Come aboard!"

Instead of the little grass basket a short rope ladder landed on the foredeck of the gondola. Alessandro laid his oar along the deck and laid hold of the chains of the fishing boat. Todaro put his hand in his pocket and produced a handful of florins which he emptied into Alessandro's pocket.

"This is just a token of what you have earned," he told the gondolier, "and we will speak of this again. Meanwhile keep yourself and that imp of a brother of yours out of trouble. Lie low for a space after this. I'll send you a message from Italy. And Alessandro, look to the Matteos. They are old and they have not earned the love of the authorities.

Alessandro took one hand off the chains for a moment and patted del Doria's shoulder.

"A pleasure to serve the Signor," he said formally and Mary could see the gleam of his teeth as he smiled, "and a joy to serve the Signorina. Good luck go with you both."

Todaro edged along the narrow strip of deck beside the canopy and bent over to help Mary out of the shelter and up the ladder. A dark and powerfully fishy shape who turned out later to be Giacomo lent a hand to help her scramble over the bulwark. Todaro followed nimbly and Alessandro pushed off at once. Mary leaned over and called out to him.

"My love to Angelo. Tell him I too wish he were ten years older!"

"Now what kind of a slur is that?" wondered Todaro close at her side.

Alessandro laughed in the darkness and saluted her with his oar before he disappeared from sight.

"In here with you," said Giacomo, "we must hoist sail and in here you will be safe."

'Here' was a crude shelter on the afterpart of the boat. It contained two boxes and a pile of nets which smelt powerfully. From one of the boxes Giacomo produced a bottle of that terrifying brandy which the Venetians called Little Champagne or Schiampagnino and two tin mugs. From the planks of the roof a lantern hung swaying on a hook.

"In an hour there will be soup," he announced, "meanwhile comfort your hearts with this."

Outside there was a creaking and a clatter of wood as Giacomo and his son hauled the gaff up the mast. The canvas of the great triangular sail rattled and clattered in the breeze. A thump on the deck indicated that the rock which served for an anchor had been swung inboard. Todaro took the bottle and poured a little into the mugs. The boat ceased its monotonous rising and falling, as Giacomo's son sheeted in the sail and set her reaching across the wind towards the Isola di Santa Elena.

"To our happy return," said Todaro and drank. Mary followed suit and choked over the fiery spirit. Todaro moved to take the mug from her but lurched against the box as the boat heeled and nearly knocked her over altogether. They grabbed at each other to steady themselves, Todaro cursing cheerfully at the boat's antics and Mary laughing and coughing. Giacomo put his head through the canvas curtain which served for a door and grinned at them.

"Put out that damned light," he advised, "I can hear a guard boat out in the narrows."

Mary found herself in total darkness. There was a low-pitched warning from Giacomo at the wheel, the *Bellissima* righted and then there was a rush and a clatter as the sail swung over. *Bellissima* heeled over on the other tack. Mary, unused to small boats, lost her footing again, staggered down to port and was brought to her knees on the pile of stinking nets. At that point she could forget the smell and saw them as a refuge. Above the working and creaking of *Bellissima* she could hear men talking on a boat nearby. Suddenly she heard one of the talkers call out. A voice yelled "Heave to!" and there was the unmistakable hiss and pop of a firework. A weird blue light filtered into the cabin. Todaro peered out through the curtain.

"Heave to!" came the order again and there was a musket-shot to reinforce the order. Mary's heart sank and her visions of safety faded like the blue light. Before it was quite gone she saw Todaro slip out of the cabin. When all was pitch dark again the *Bellissima* righted herself once more and with a healthy snap of canvas heeled over on to the old tack, but this time she did not stay there but wore right round, freeing off until she was running before the wind along the shore of the island.

It was a neat manoeuvre and gained them a good lead before the guard-boat sent up another blue light and with a volley of curses audible down-wind weathered right round on to the same course as their quarry. Mary emerged from the cabin as the light died.

"Where's Giacomo going?" she asked, "Can he get away from it?"

"Through the narrows and into the lagoon."

"That's not where we're going now . . . isn't that running into a trap?"

"Not when you know these waters as well as Giacomo."

Mary felt rather than saw the land on her right hand, but she knew they must be close to the shore. Giacomo hardened in a little and the boat brushed past a crooked pole with a bundle of brushwood on the top.

"That's supposed to mark the channel," explained Todaro, "and we, so far as I can judge, are on the wrong side of it."

"We have no fish and the tide is making," said Giacomo as if in extenuation for this breach of maritime good sense. Todaro grunted acknowledgement but Mary could feel how tense he was.

He pulled her close, a gesture so natural and welcome that she did not question it. Another marker-post loomed up this time a lot farther away. Todaro shifted restlessly and Mary felt a change in the gait of the boat. She seemed to hesitate like a woman trying to cross a busy street, dash on for a moment or two and then hesitate again. The gaff clattered against the mast and this time Mary could hear a faint hushing sound and realised that the keel of the boat was brushing over the sand.

"There is a nice new shoal here," said Giacomo calmly, "but we should get over it . . ."

Bellissima picked up speed again. Just at that minute the third rocket went up. The guard-boat was about twenty lengths behind, all sail spread in that brisk breeze. Giacomo grinned contentedly.

"She draws half a metre more than *Bellissima*," he observed and gave the tiller a slight push. "Sheet in boy! We'll beat back through the narrows and so out to sea."

The sail was hauled inwards, the sheet creaking through the blocks and once more *Bellissima* heeled to the wind, the water bubbling and chuckling at her forefoot. Todaro drew Mary to the weather side of the cabin. The guard-boat, suspicious of her quarry's change of course sent up a fourth rocket and thus illuminated her own downfall. She struck the shoal going at about four knots, the top of her mast snapped like a twig and the boat pressed down by her spread of canvas heeled right over on her beam-ends.

Bellissima, back in the deep channel, danced past the wreck and Giacomo made a regrettable gesture of triumph.

Later that night when the wind had died and *Bellissima* was becalmed well out in the Adriatic waiting for the wind which springs up after sunrise, Giacomo's son lit a fire in the tiny iron basket which stood on a square of bricks on the foredeck. Over this they heated a pot of squassetto into which they all dipped with a communal spoon and chunks of stale bread. Afterwards Mary and Todaro, reluctant to re-enter the stinking cabin leaned side by side on the bulwark and looked eastward.

"Istria's over there," he told her, "we'll make Rovigno in the morning."

The light was growing in the east. He pulled at the dishevelled black wig.

"You can surely rid yourself of that now?"

Mary hauled it off and pulled off the net which held her own hair confined beneath it. It tumbled over her shoulders as if it was glad of its freedom. Todaro took the wig out of her hand and dangled it over the silky water.

"I thought," he said calmly, "I thought we could be married

in Rovigno. After a while we will go to Milano. I have friends there who are working to be rid of the Austrian ..."

He looked at her but she said nothing although her heart was beating painfully fast.

"Why so silent?" he asked. "Don't you care for the idea?"

He turned her gently to face him.

"You know I had the notion, I cannot think why, that you might not altogether dislike it."

"No," said Mary, her eyes on his waistcoat buttons.

"No?" he said, a little uncertainly.

"I meant," she told him looking up for the first time and smiling rather mischievously, "no ... I do not altogether dislike it."

He took her hand in a painful grip.

"You know I could spend half my life in jail," he warned, "that I might even meet an untoward end?"

"I would, of course, endeavour to circumvent such a misfortune," Mary said primly.

"You might even succeed," he agreed. "I could be beggared."

"How fortunate," Mary observed, "that I can always command a frugal living for us both."

"I believe you would. Your house will always be filled with doubtful characters, adventurers, soldiers of fortune, politicians ..."

"I think I would prefer them to the vapid," said Mary, her eyes on the white mountains of Istria gilded by the rising sun.

"You will have to endure a printing press in your cellar and conspirators in your drawing room. The police will watch your comings and goings ..."

"It seems to me," said Mary, "that you are at some pains to disgust me with the idea. I shall begin to think that you wish me to cry off."

Todaro dispelled such a mistaken notion in a manner which left Mary in no doubt of his feelings in the matter, and which won the open admiration of the crew of the *Bellissima*.

"Has it occurred to you," asked Mary, when she had regained a degree of composure, "that Venice may soon be free of Austria?

Events in Germany might lead one to suppose ... what will you do then for an occupation?"

"I would be left at liberty to devote myself entirely to you," he returned, "unless, of course, you discover a desire in yourself to be married to a Prime Minister?"

He looked at her hopefully.

"I have few political ambitions," she told him.

"In that case," he said mournfully, "we will live in happy seclusion between my estates in the Veneto-Giulia and Venice and rear a large family of hopeful children ... while I eat the bitter bread of idleness."

"No one with a large and hopeful family can be idle," said Mary.

"But we will employ a first-class governess," he returned. "And of course, who knows, my sons may take an interest in politics and I may live vicariously through them as they scale the heights that you deny me."

He shook his head at the prospect.

"You seem to forget, they will also be my children. I confidently expect that half of them at least will wish to be singers like their grandfather, their grandmother and their aunt..."

"A bagatelle," he shrugged, "their talent can serve in either situation. Politics are opera buffa without the music."

"Enough," said Mary and put up her hand which was promptly taken and kissed, "I see my fate is sealed. There is no escape."

"None," he agreed enthusiastically.

He hurled the black wig as far as he could into the sea.

"The current sets into Venice," he observed. "I wonder what Venice will make of that object."

"If I am any judge of them," replied Mary with feeling, "squassetto."